THE HEAD OF PROFESSOR DOWELL

By Alexander Belyaev

Translation and cover art by Maria K. with images provided by 123RF

Editing by PubRight Manuscript Services

Copyright © 2012 by TSK Group LLC

TABLE OF CONTENTS

THE FIRST MEETING

"Sit down, please."

Marie Lauran settled into a deep leather armchair.

While Professor Kern opened the envelope and read the recommendation letter, she quickly surveyed the study.

What a gloomy room! But it would be nice for reading and working, as there was nothing to distract one's attention. A lamp with an opaque shade lit only the desk covered with books, manuscripts and proof runs. One's eye could barely distinguish the imposing furniture of black oak. The wallpaper was dark as were the drapes. Only the gilded book bindings glinted in their heavy book cases. A long pendulum of an antique wall clock moved smoothly and regularly.

Shifting her gaze to Kern, Lauran smiled despite herself: the professor himself entirely corresponded to the style of his study. Kern's dark heavy figure, seemingly carved from oak, matched the furniture. The large horn-rimmed glasses looked like two clock faces. His eyes, the color of gray ash, moved like pendulums as he went from one line of the letter to the next. Angular nose, a straight linear cut of the eyes and mouth, and square protruding chin made his face look like a stylized decorative mask created by a cubist sculptor.

"A mask like that would look good above the mantle," Lauran thought.

1

"My colleague Sabatier spoke highly of you. Yes, I do need an assistant. You are a medical school graduate? Excellent. Forty franks per day. You get paid every week. You shall receive breakfast and lunch here. But I insist upon one condition."

Drumming with his dry fingers on the desk, Professor Kern asked an unexpected question, "Can you keep your mouth shut? All women are chatty. You are a woman – that is bad enough. You are beautiful – that is even worse."

"What does it have to do…"

"Everything. A beautiful woman is twice the woman. This means she possesses twice the amount of all the feminine drawbacks. You might have a husband, a friend, a fiancé. And then all the secrets go to hell."

"But…"

"But nothing! You must be as mute as a fish. You must say nothing about anything you see and hear here. Do you accept this condition? I must warn you; insubordination will have extremely unpleasant consequences for you. Extremely unpleasant."

Lauran was confused and curious.

"I agree, as long as there is nothing…"

"Criminal, you mean to say? You may rest assured. And you are in no danger of any kind of responsibility. Are your nerves in order?"

"I am well."

Professor Kern nodded.

"Are there any alcoholics, neurotics, epileptics or madmen in your family?"

"No."

Kern nodded again.

His dry pointy finger pressed the button for the electrical servant bell.

The door opened noiselessly.

In the dim room, Lauran saw, as if developed on a photographic plate, the whites of the eyes, followed by glints of an African's ebony skin. His black hair and suit were almost invisible against the dark door drapes.

"John! Show Mademoiselle Lauran the laboratory."

The African nodded, inviting her to follow, and opened the second door.

Lauran entered a completely dark room.

A switch clicked, and bright light from four frosted half-globes flooded the room. Lauran covered her eyes. After the half-darkness of the gloomy study the whiteness of the walls was blinding. Glass doors of cases sparkled, as did the shiny surgical tools within. Devices that Lauran was unfamiliar with gleamed with cold steel and aluminum. Warm, yellow light spots rested upon polished copper. Pipes, spirals, beakers, glass cylinders, glass, rubber, and metal were everywhere.

In the middle of the room stood a large dissecting table. Next to the table was a glass box with a human heart pulsing within. Tubes connected the heart to various cylinders.

3

Lauran turned her head and suddenly saw something that made her shudder as if from an electric shock.

A human head was looking at her – just the head without a body.

It was attached to a square sheet of glass. The sheet was supported by four shiny metal legs. Tubes were inserted into the cut arteries and veins, went through openings in the glass and connected, either in pairs or separately, to a series of cylinders. A large thick tube came out of the throat and was connected to the largest container in the room. It and other cylinders had valves, pressure and temperature gages, and other attachments Lauran could not identify.

The head was looking at Lauran carefully and sadly, blinking slowly. There was no doubt: the head was alive, separated from the body, with its own independent and conscious life.

Despite the striking impression, Lauran could not help but notice that the head looked remarkably like that of the recently deceased famous surgeon, Professor Dowell, who was well-known for his experiments of reviving organs separated from a body. Lauran has been to his brilliant public lectures many times, and remembered well this high forehead, handsome profile, thick wavy hair shot with silver, blue eyes... Yes, it was the head of Professor Dowell. His lips and nose were thinner, his temples and cheeks – dryer, his eyes were set deeper and his once-white skin now had the dark yellow tinge of a mummy. But the eyes were filled with life and thought.

Lauran was entranced and could not look away from these blue eyes.

The head silently moved its lips.

That was too much for Lauran's nerves. She was on the verge of fainting. The African took her elbow and led her out of the laboratory.

"This is terrible, terrible," Lauran repeated as she returned to her seat.

Professor Kern silently drummed his fingers on the desk.

"Tell me, is it really the head?"

"Of Professor Dowell? Yes, it's his head. The head of my respected colleague brought back to life by me. Unfortunately, I could only resurrect the head. But one cannot accomplish everything from the first try. Poor Dowell suffered from an incurable illness. Before he died, he bequeathed his body for scientific experiments he and I conducted together. 'My entire life was devoted to science. My death might as well be devoted to it too. I would rather have a colleague pick through my body than an earthworm.' Such was Professor Dowell's will. And I received his body. I managed to not only revive his heart and head, but also his consciousness, his 'soul' so to speak. What's so terrible about that? People consider death terrible. Hasn't resurrection been a centuries-long dream of humankind?"

"I would prefer death to such resurrection."

Professor Kern gestured with his hand.

"Yes, it has certain inconveniences for the resurrected. Poor Dowell couldn't show up in public in such… an incomplete state. That is why we are keeping this experiment secret. I am saying 'we', because such is the wish of Dowell himself. Besides, the experiment is not yet complete."

"How did Professor Dowell, or rather his head, express this desire? Can the head talk?"

Professor Kern seemed taken aback for a moment.

"No. Professor Dowell's head cannot talk. But it can hear, understand and reply by using his facial muscles."

To change the subject, Professor Kern asked, "Well then, do you accept my offer? Excellent. I shall expect you tomorrow at nine o'clock in the morning. But remember: silence, silence, and silence."

THE MYSTERY OF THE FORBIDDEN VALVE

Marie Lauran's life was never easy. She was seventeen when her father died. Marie had to take care of her sick mother. The limited sum left by her father did not last very long, and she had to go to school and work to support the household. For several years she worked as a night issue editor for a newspaper. Having received her medical degree, she searched for a job in vain. She had offers to go to the deadly regions of New Guinea in the middle of a yellow fever epidemic. But Marie did not want to either go there with her sick mother or leave her mother behind. Professor Kern's offer was the only option for her.

Despite the strange circumstances of the job, she agreed almost without hesitation.

Lauran did not know that, prior to interviewing her, Professor Kern made thorough inquiries about her.

She had been working for Kern for two weeks. Her duties were not difficult. She had to watch the devices supporting the head's life. At night, she was replaced by John.

Professor Kern explained to her how to use the valves on the various cylinders. Pointing at the large reservoir with the thick pipe connected to the head's throat, Kern absolutely forbade her to open its valve.

"If you turn the valve, the head will be instantly killed. At some point I shall explain to you the feeding system for the head and the

7

purpose of this cylinder. In the meantime, it's enough for you to know how to use the other equipment."

Nevertheless, Kern was in no rush to provide these explanations.

A small thermometer was inserted deep into one of the head's nostrils. At certain times, it had to be pulled out and the temperature recorded. The cylinders also had pressure and temperature gages. Lauren had to monitor their liquid temperature and pressure. The well-tuned equipment gave her no trouble, working with all the precision of a Swiss watch. The particularly sensitive device set against the head's temple monitored its pulse and was attached to a drawing device, drawing a continuous graph. The ribbon was replaced every day. The contents of the cylinders were replenished in Lauran's absence.

Marie gradually became used to the head and even grew fond of it.

When Lauran entered the laboratory every morning, with her cheeks flushed from a brisk walk in the fresh air, the head smiled weakly, and its eyelids trembled as the sign of greeting.

The head could not speak. However, Lauran had quickly learned its sign language, albeit a very limited one. The lowering of the eyelids meant "yes", the raising meant "no". The noiselessly moving lips were also somewhat helpful.

"How are you doing today?" Lauran asked.

The head smiled with a "shadow of a smile" and lowered its eyelids, "Very well, thank you."

8

"Did you sleep well?"

The same response.

As she asked questions, Lauren quickly performed her morning duties. She checked the devices, temperature, pulse, and made notes in the log. Then, with the greatest care, she washed the head's face with a sponge soaked in a solution of water and alcohol and wiped the ears with sterile cotton. She plucked a bit of cotton stuck to the eyelashes and washed the eyes, nose and mouth – there were special tubes for that. She brushed the hair.

Her hands touched the head deftly and gently. The head's face bore an expression of pleasure.

"It's wonderful out today," Lauran said. "The sky is so blue. The air is frosty and clear. You can't help but breathe as deeply as you can. Look at the sun – it shines as if it's already spring."

The corners of Professor Dowell's lips drooped sadly. His eyes glanced sadly at the window, and then returned to Lauran.

She blushed, annoyed with herself. Usually, with her instincts of a sensitive woman, Lauran avoided talking about anything that was unreachable for the head and could remind it of the deficiencies of its existence.

Marie felt a kind of motherly compassion toward the head, as if it was a helpless child, deprived by nature.

"Well, let us get to work!" Lauran said quickly, trying to cover her mistake.

In the mornings, before Professor Kern's arrival, the head read extensively. Lauran brought in a stack of all the latest medical

9

journals and books and showed them to the head. The head glanced at the titles. When it reached the right article, it moved its eyebrows. Lauran set the magazine onto a stand and the head read. Lauran became used to following the head's eyes and guessing when to turn the page.

When it wanted to make a mark in the margin, the head made a sign, and Lauran ran her finger over the lines, watching the head's eyes and marking the passage with a pencil.

Lauran did not know why the head wanted her to make these marks, and she couldn't hope to receive an explanation through the head's limited sign language, so she never asked.

One time, however, she was passing through Professor Kern's study when he was absent, and saw on the desk the magazines with the paragraphs she marked as instructed by the head. The marked passages were copied down in Professor Kern's hand onto a separate sheet of paper. That caused Lauran to wonder.

Once she got to thinking about it, Marie couldn't help but ask. Perhaps, the head would find a way to explain.

"Tell me, why do we mark certain passages in the scientific articles?"

An expression of displeasure and impatience appeared on Professor Dowell's face. The head look expressively at Lauran, then at the valve with the tube leading to the head's throat, and lifted its eyebrows twice. That meant a request. Lauran realized that the head wanted her to open that forbidden valve. It wasn't the first time the head appealed to her with the same request. But

Lauran interpreted the head's request in her own way: apparently, the head wanted to finish its hopeless existence. And Lauran didn't dare open the valve. She didn't want to cause the head's death, nor did she want the responsibility or to lose her job.

"No, no," Lauren replied fearfully to the head's request. "If I open that valve, you shall die. I don't want to, I cannot, and I do not dare kill you."

The head's face twisted with impatience and the sense of helplessness.

It quickly raised its eyelids and eyes three times.

"No, no, no. I will not die!" Lauran interpreted. She hesitated.

The head started moving its lips silently, and Lauran realized that it tried saying, "Open, open, please!"

Lauran's curiosity was excited in the extreme. She felt that there was a mystery behind all this.

The head's eyes were filled with boundless sadness. Its eyes asked, begged, demanded. It seemed that all power of human thought, all the strain of will were focused in its gaze.

Lauran made a decision.

Her heart beating fast, her hand shaking, she carefully opened the valve.

Instantly, there was a hiss in the head's throat. Lauran head a weak, dull, crackling voice as shaky as a broken record player, "Thank... you."

The forbidden valve opened way to the compressed air. As it passed through the head's throat, the air moved the vocal cords and enabled the head to speak. The throat muscles and ligaments could no longer work properly, and the air passed through the air with a hiss, when the head was not speaking. The cuts in neck nerves violated the normal work of the vocal cords and gave the voice the dull, trembling quality.

The head's face expressed satisfaction.

At that moment, there were footsteps in the study and the sound of the door being unlocked (the laboratory was always locked from the study). Lauran barely managed to close the valve. The hissing in the head's throat stopped.

Professor Kern came in.

THE HEAD SPEAKS

A week passed since Lauran discovered the secret of the big valve.

During that time the friendship between Lauran and the head became even stronger. During those times, when Professor Kern left for the university or the clinic, Lauran opened the valve, letting a weak stream of air into the head's throat and enabling it to talk in a whisper. Lauran spoke quietly too. They were afraid of being overheard by John.

Their conversations clearly had a positive effect upon Professor Dowell. His eyes became livelier and the careworn creases between his eyebrows smoothed out.

The head spoke much and willingly, as if rewarding itself for the time of forced silence.

The night before Lauran dreamed of Professor Dowell's head in her sleep and when she woke up she thought, "Does the head itself dream?"

"Dreams..." the head whispered quietly. "Yes, I can dream. And I don't know whether I get more grief or joy from them. In my dreams I see myself healthy and full of energy, so when I wake up I feel doubly robbed. Robbed physically and emotionally. After all, I am deprived of everything that other people have. All I have left is the ability think. 'I think therefore I am'," the head quoted Descartes with a bitter smile, "I am..."

"What do you dream about?"

"I have never dreamed of myself as I am now. I see myself the way I used to be. I see my family and friends. I recently dreamed about my late wife and re-lived the spring of our romance. Betty came to me as a patient – she hurt her leg when getting out of a car. Our first meeting was in my exam room. Somehow, we became very close almost right away. After her fourth visit, I asked her to look at the portrait of my fiancée on the desk. 'I shall marry her if she says yes,' I said. She came to the desk and saw a small mirror; she picked it up and looked at it, then laughed and said, 'I think she will.' In a week we were married. This scene passed before me in my dreams just recently. Betty died here, in Paris. You know, I came here from America as a war surgeon. Then I was offered a university post, and I stayed here. And then I stayed to be next to the beloved grave. My wife was an amazing woman."

The head's face grew brighter with memories, but then darkened again.

"This time seems so infinitely long ago!"

The head pondered. Air hissed quietly in its throat.

"Last night, I dreamed about my son. I wish I could see him one more time. But I don't dare subject him to this. I am dead for him."

"You have a grown son? Where is he now?"

"Yes, he is a grown man. He is the same age as you, or a bit older. He graduated from university. Presently, he is in England, with his mother's sister. I wish I didn't dream. But it's not just the dreams," the head continued after a pause, "that torture me. When

14

I am awake, I am tricked by phantom sensations. As strange as it may seem, sometimes I imagine I can feel my body. I suddenly want to take a deep breath, stretch, open my arms, like a person who's been sitting for too long. And sometimes I feel arthritis pain in my left leg. Isn't it funny? Although, you are a doctor, so you probably understand how it works. The pain is so real that I look down despite myself, and, of course, see the empty space under the glass and the stone tiles of the floor. At times I feel as if I am about to have an asthma attack, and then I am almost happy about my 'life after death', which at least eliminates that problem. It's all in the purely reflexive activity of brain cells, once connected to the workings of the body."

"It's terrible!" Lauran said.

"Yes, it is. It's strange, when I was alive I thought I lived solely by the power of thought. Somehow, I didn't notice my body; I was always neck-deep in my scientific research. And only after I had lost my body, I understood how much I lost with it. Now, more than ever, I think about the smell of flowers, fragrant hay, the woods, long walks, the noise of sea waves. I haven't lost my senses of smell, touch and the rest, but I am cut off from the entire world teeming with sensations. The smell of hay is only good in the field, when it is associated with a thousand other things: the scent of the woods, the beauty of sunset, the birdsong. Artificial smells could never replace the real ones. The smell of perfume *Rose* without the flower? It's just as bad as the smell of pate for a hungry person, without the pate itself. Having lost my body, I have lost the

15

world — the entire boundless, beautiful world filled with things I have never noticed, things I could pick up and touch, and at the same time feel my own body, the sense of myself. Oh, I would have gladly given up this fantastic existence for the joy of sensing the weight of a simple stone in my hand! If you only knew how much pleasure I derive from the touch of the sponge, when you wash my face in the morning. Touch is the only thing that still connects me to the world of real things. All I can do on my own is touch the tip of my tongue to my lips when they feel dry."

That evening Lauran came home absent-minded and agitated. Her elderly mother prepared tea and some cold snacks for her, as usual, but Marie didn't touch the sandwiches, downed a glass of tea with lemon and rose to go to her room. Her mother looked at her carefully.

"Is something wrong, Marie?" the old woman said. "Perhaps, some problems at work?"

"No, it's nothing, Mom, I am just tired and have a headache. I'll go to bed early and all will be well."

Her mother didn't stop her, but sighed and fell deep into thought.

Ever since Marie accepted the job with Professor Kern, she was changed. She became nervous and secretive. Mother and daughter were always very close. They had no secrets from each other. But now, there was one. Madam Lauran felt that her daughter was hiding something from her. To her mother's questions about the job, Marie gave very brief and vague answers.

"Professor Kern has a clinic at home for particularly interesting patients. I take care of them."

"What sort of patients?"

"All sorts. Some of them are very difficult cases." Marie frowned and changed the subject.

The old woman was not satisfied by these answers. She even started making careful inquiries, but was unable to find out anything that she didn't already know from her daughter.

"Is she in love with Kern, and he doesn't return her feelings?" the woman thought. But she instantly disagreed with herself; her daughter would have never concealed anything like that from her. And besides, wasn't Marie the prettiest girl? And Kern was a bachelor. If Marie fell in love with him, surely Kern couldn't resist. There wasn't another Marie in the whole world. No, there was something else... And the old lady couldn't sleep for a long time, tossing and turning between her perfectly fluffed pillows.

Marie couldn't sleep either. Having turned off the light to make her mother think that she was asleep, Marie sat on her bed with her eyes wide open. She remembered everything the head told her and tried to imagine herself in its place: she touched her tongue to her lips, her palate and her teeth and thought, "This is all the head can do. It can bite its lips and the tip of its tongue. It can move its eyebrows. It can roll its eyes, open and close them.

Its mouth and its eyes – that is all it can move. Perhaps it can slightly scrunch the skin on its forehead. And nothing else..."

Marie opened and closed her eyes and made faces. If only her mother could see her now! The poor old woman would have thought that her daughter went mad.

Then Marie grabbed her shoulders, knees and arms, patted her neck, ran her fingers through her thick hair and whispered, "My God! I am so lucky! I have so much! I am rich! And I had no idea!"

The tired young body demanded sleep. Marie's eyes drooped shut. And then she saw Dowell's head. The head gazed at her attentively and sadly. It pulled off its table and flew through the air. Marie ran away from it. Kern attacked the head, like a hawk. There were winding hallways and tight doors. Marie hurried to open them, but the doors didn't yield and Kern was catching up to the head. The head whistled and hissed right over her ear. Marie felt as if she was suffocating. Her heart was pounding and its beating reverberated through her entire body. Cold shivers ran down her spine. She kept opening more and more doors. It was terrible!

"Marie! Marie! What is wrong? Wake up. Marie! You are moaning."

It was no longer a dream. Her mother was standing at the head of her bed and anxiously patting her hair.

"It's alright, mom. I had a bad dream, is all."

"You've been having more and more bad dreams lately, my darling."

The old woman left with a sigh, and Marie remained awake for a while longer, lying in bed with her eyes wide open and her heart still beating fast.

"My nerves are getting worse and worse," she whispered quietly and fell soundly asleep.

DEATH OR MURDER?

Once, when leafing through medical magazines before bed, Lauran ran into an article written by Professor Kern about his scientific research. In that article Kern referred to the works of other scientists in the same area. All these excerpts were taken from the scientific journals and books and matched exactly the ones that Lauran underlined, following the head's instructions during their morning studies.

The next day, the moment she had an opportunity to talk to the head, Lauran asked, "What does Professor Kern do in the laboratory in my absence?"

After some hesitation the head replied, "We continue our work together."

"You mean you marked all those articles for him? Are you aware that he publishes your joined work as the sole author?"

"I guessed as much."

"But that is outrageous! How can you stand it?"

"What can I do?"

"If you can't, then I'll do something!" Lauran exclaimed angrily.

"Quiet… No need… It would be ridiculous to argue about the authorship in my position. Money? What for? Fame? What will it give me? And then… if all this comes to light, our work will never be finished. And I am very interested in having it finished. I admit, I want to see the result of my labor."

Lauran thought it over.

"Yes, a man like Kern is capable of anything," she said quietly. "Professor Kern told me, when he was hiring me, that you died of an incurable illness and bequeathed your body for scientific work. Is that true?"

"It is difficult for me to talk about it. I may be mistaken. It is true but, perhaps... not entirely true. He and I worked together on reviving human organs taken out of a fresh corpse. Kern was my assistant. The end goal of my work at the time was reviving a head separated from the body. I had finished all of the preparations. We have already revived heads of animals, but decided not to publicize our results until we managed to revive and demonstrate a human head. Shortly before that last experiment, which I had no doubt would have been successful, I handed to Kern the manuscript with all of my work to prepare for publication. At the same time we were working on another problem, and were also approaching resolution. At that time I had a terrible asthma attack – one of those illnesses I, as a scientist, did my best to defeat. It and I have long been enemies. It was all a matter of time: which one of us would come out on top in the end. I knew it could defeat me. And I really did bequeath my body for scientific work, even though I had no idea that it would be my head to be revived. And then... during that last attack, Kern was next to me and provided first aid. He injected me with adrenaline. Perhaps... the dose was too high, or the asthma may have done its job."

"And then?"

"Asphyxiation, short agony and death, which for me was merely a loss of consciousness. And then I experienced a very strange transition. Consciousness returned to me very slowly. I think I was awakened by the acute pain around my neck. The pain gradually diminished. At the time I did not realize what it meant. When Kern and I experimented with reviving dogs' heads, we noticed that they experienced extremely sharp pain right after waking up. The heads thrashed so hard on their platters, that some of the tubes came out from the blood vessels, through which the heads were being fed. Then I proposed anesthetizing the cut. To keep it from drying out and becoming infected, the dog's neck was set into a special solution called Ringen-Lock-Dowell. The solution contained the feeding, antiseptic and anesthetizing agents. My own neck was submerged into the same solution. Without that precaution I could have died for the second time, like the dogs' heads did in our earliest experiments. But, as I said, it wasn't what I was thinking at that moment. Everything was swimming as if someone woke me up after a strong inebriation, with alcohol still affecting my senses. But a happy thought still flashed through my brain, that if I had at least a shred of consciousness, then I wasn't dead.

"Before I opened my eyes, I considered the strange points of that last attack. Usually, my asthma attacks stopped suddenly. Sometimes there was a residual shortness of breath. But I have never passed out during an attack. That was new. Also new was the pain around my neck. Another strange thing was: I felt that I

22

was not breathing, but I was not suffocating either. I tried to take a breath and couldn't. I had lost the sense of my chest. I couldn't expand my chest cavity even thought I was straining my chest muscles as hard as I could, or so I thought. 'That is odd,' I thought, 'I must be asleep and dreaming…' I opened my eyes with difficulty. It was dark. There was a vague noise in my ears. I closed my eyes again.

"You know, when someone dies, his senses do not fade away all at once. At first, the person loses the sense of taste, then his vision, then his hearing. Apparently, the restoration took place in reverse. After some time, I raised my eyelids again and saw dim light. It was as if I was very deep underwater. Then the greenish murk started dissipating and I could vaguely see Kern's face before me and heard his voice fairly clearly, 'Are you back? I am very happy to see you alive once again.' With an effort of will, I forced my consciousness to clear faster. I looked down and saw a table right under my chin – that was before we had this little table, and there was a regular table, similar to a kitchen table that Kern adapted for the experiment. I wanted to look behind me but couldn't turn my head. Next to the table was the dissecting table. On it was someone's headless body. I looked at it and the body looked familiar, even though it did not have a head and its chest cavity was open. Someone's heart was beating in a glass box nearby. I looked at Kern in confusion. I still couldn't understand why my head was on a table and why I couldn't see my body. I wanted to reach out with my hand and couldn't. 'What happened?'

I wanted to ask Kern but only moved my lips. He looked at me and smiled. 'Don't you recognize it?' he asked nodding at the dissecting table. 'It's your own body. You are now rid of asthma for good.' He could still joke! And then I knew. I admit, at the first moment I wanted to scream, pull from the table, kill myself and Kern. Or rather... I knew in my mind that I should have been enraged, screaming and protesting, but I was struck by the icy calm that came over me. Perhaps, I was outraged but it was as if I was looking at myself from the outside. Something had shifted in my psyche. I frowned and remained silent. Could I really become as agitated as before, when my old heart was beating in a glass container and my new heart was nothing but a motor?"

Lauran gazed at the head in horror.

"And after that... you still continue working with him. Had it not been for him, you would have conquered the asthma and would have remained a complete person. He is a thief and a murderer, and you are helping him rise to the heights of glory. You are working for him. He feeds upon your mind like a parasite; he made you into some sort of a generator of creative thought and is now making money and fame with it. And you! What does he give you? What kind of life is this? You have been deprived of everything. You are a poor remain, in which desires can still live, to your own detriment. Kern had stolen the entire world from you. Forgive me, but I do not understand you. How can you work for him so obligingly and without complaint?"

The head smiled sadly.

"A head's revolt? That would have been sensational. But what could I do? After all, I am deprived even of the last human choice of committing suicide."

"But you could refuse to work with him!"

"I have been through that, if you must know. But my revolt was not caused by the fact that Kern takes advantage of my thinking ability. After all, who cares what the author's name is? The important thing is for the idea to enter the world and do its job. I revolted because it was difficult for me to get used to my new existence. I wished for death instead of life. Let me tell you what happened to me around that time. I was alone in the laboratory once. Suddenly, a big black beetle flew in through the window. Where did it come from in the middle of a huge city? I have no idea. Perhaps, it was brought in by a car coming back from a suburban picnic. The beetle circled above me and landed onto the glass top of my table, right next to me. I moved my eyes to watch the disgusting insect, unable to get rid of it. The beetle's legs slipped on the glass as it slowly approached me. I don't know if you can fully understand me. I have always had a particular dislike for this sort of insect. I would have never touched it. And I was helpless even before such an insignificant enemy. All my head was for was a convenient platform for takeoff. And it continued crawling toward me, its legs rustling. With some effort it managed to grab the hairs of my beard. It thrashed around, tangled in the hair, but stubbornly climbed higher. It crawled over my lips, up the left side of my nose, over my shut left eye, until it finally made it to

25

my forehead, then fell back onto the glass and then on the floor. It was a trifling incident. But it struck me deeply. And when Professor Kern returned, I absolutely refused to continue working with him. I knew he wouldn't dare demonstrate my head in public. And he wouldn't keep me without any benefit to himself, for I was a piece of evidence against him. And he would kill me. Such was my plan.

"We struggled. He used some pretty cruel measures. Once, late in the evening, he came in with an electrical device, attached electrodes to my temples and addressed me. He stood before me, with his arms crossed on his chest, and spoke in a very gentle, soothing tone, like a real inquisitor. 'My dear colleague,' he began, 'we are alone here, eye to eye, behind heavy stone walls. Although, even if they were thinner, it wouldn't make any difference, because you cannot scream. You are entirely in my power. I can inflict the most terrible torture upon you and escape unharmed. But why? We are both scientists and understand each other. I know that things have not been easy for you, but that is not my fault. I need you and I cannot set you free from this difficult existence, even as you yourself cannot escape from me. Why don't we make a truce? You shall continue our studies...' I moved my eyebrows to decline, and my lips whispered, 'No!' 'You are making me very sad,' he said. 'Would you like a cigarette? I know you cannot enjoy it to the fullest, because you have no lungs through which nicotine can permeate the blood, but at least you could have the comfort of a familiar sensation.' He pulled out two cigarettes, smoked one himself and stuck another one into my mouth. I spat it out with great pleasure! 'Very well, colleague,' he said in the same unperturbed voice, 'you are forcing me to use extreme measures.' He turned on the current. It was as if a searing hot drill pierced my brain. 'How do you feel?' he asked gently, as if I was his patient. 'A headache? Perhaps you would like to cure it? All you need to do is...' 'No!' my lips replied. 'Very, very sad. I shall have to increase the current slightly. You are greatly disappointing me.' And he turned the current up so much that I felt as if my head was on fire. The pain was intolerable. I clenched my teeth. I felt as if I would faint and I very much wanted to. But, unfortunately, I didn't. I closed my eyes and pressed my lips together. Kern kept smoking, breathing smoke into my face, and continued slowly roasting my head. He no longer reasoned with me. When I opened my eyes slightly, I saw that he was enraged by my resistance. 'Damn you! If I didn't have such great need of your brains, I would have fried them and fed them to my pincher. Stubborn old man!' He unceremoniously pulled the electrodes off my head and left. However, it was too soon to celebrate.

"Soon he returned and started combining the solutions that feed my head with irritating substances that caused me most terrible pains. And when I winced, he asked me, 'Well then, colleague, have you decided? Still no?' I was unmoved. He left even more enraged, showering me with curses. I was triumphant. Kern didn't come back to the laboratory for several days, and I

27

was expecting to die any day. On the fifth day he returned, whistling a tune, as if nothing happened. Without looking at me he continued working. I watched him for two or three days, without offering to participate. But the work couldn't help but interest me. When he made several mistakes in the course of some experiments, mistakes that could have been fateful to all of our efforts, I couldn't stand it and signed him to turn on the valve. 'About time!' he said with a pleased smile, and turned on the air. I explained his errors and have been leading the work ever since. I guess he turned out to be cleverer than I."

VICTIMS OF THE CITY

Ever since Lauran had discovered the head's secret, she came to hate Kern. And the feeling grew stronger with each passing day. She fell asleep with it and woke up with it. She saw Kern in her nightmares. She was sick with hatred. Whenever she saw Kern she barely kept from shouting, "Murderer!" to his face.

Her manner toward him was strained and cold.

"Kern is a terrible criminal!" Marie exclaimed, when left alone with the head. "I shall report him. I shall shout about his crimes, and I won't rest until I destroy his stolen glory and uncover all of his crimes. I won't spare myself."

"Quiet! Calm down," Dowell said. "I told you, I feel no need for revenge. But if your own ethics are upset and yearn for retribution, I cannot talk you out of it. Don't rush, however. I am asking you to wait until we finish our experiments. Right now I need Kern as much as he needs me. He cannot complete our work without me, but I cannot do it alone either. After all, that is all that's left to me. I cannot create anything new, but the work that has been started must be complete."

There were footsteps in the study.

Lauran quickly turned down the valve and sat down with a book in her hands, still outraged. Dowell's head lowered its eyelids like a person dosing off.

Professor Kern entered.

He looked at Lauran suspiciously.

"What is the matter? Are you upset by something? Is everything alright?"

"No… nothing. Everything is fine. Trouble at home."

"Let me check your pulse."

Lauran reluctantly held out her hand.

"It's elevated. Your nerves are getting the better of you. This work is difficult for emotional people. But I am pleased by you. I am doubling your salary."

"There is no need, thank you."

"No need? Who doesn't need money? After all, you are the sole provider, aren't you?'

Lauran said nothing.

"Listen. We must make some changes. We shall move Professor Dowell's head into the next room. It's only temporary, colleague, only temporary. Are you asleep?" he addressed the head. "Tomorrow, we shall have two fresh corpses with which we shall make a couple of nice talking heads and demonstrate them to the scientific society. It is time to publicize our discovery."

Kern once again gave Lauran a searching look.

To avoid showing her disdain too soon, Lauran forced herself to assume the look of indifference and asked the first question that occurred to her, "Whose corpses?"

"I do not know, and no one does. Because, right now, they are not corpses but normal, healthy people. I can tell you that with utmost certainty. I need heads from completely healthy people.

But tomorrow, they shall die. And an hour after that, they shall be right here, on the dissecting table. I shall make certain of that."

Lauran, despite the fact that she expected anything from Professor Kern, gave him such a terrified look that he became confused for a moment and then burst out laughing.

"It's quite simple. I have ordered a couple of fresh corpses at the morgue. You see, the city is nothing but a modern hell that demands daily human sacrifices. Every day, with all the immutability of the laws of nature, people die in traffic accidents, as well as in industrial and construction accidents. These ill-fated people, happy, full of energy and health, will go to bed and sleep soundly tonight, not knowing what awaits them tomorrow. Tomorrow morning, they will get up and get dressed, humming a merry tune, before leaving, as they think, to go to work but in reality – to meet their end. At the same time, at the other end of the city, their unwilling executioner will be getting ready just as happily – a truck or tram driver, perhaps. Then the victim will leave his apartment, and the executioner will set out from his garage or depot. They shall inexorably approach each other through the traffic, not knowing each other, until that fateful point of intersection. Then one of them will become distracted for a second and – voila! The statistical graphs tracking the number of traffic casualties shall get another data point. Thousands of small circumstances lead them to that one fatal point. And nevertheless, it will happen inevitably, with the precision of a clock mechanism that brings together two clock hands traveling at different speeds."

Professor Kern was never that chatty with Lauran. And why the sudden generosity? "I am doubling your salary."

"He wants to soften me up and buy me off," Lauran thought. "I think he suspects that I have either guessed or already know a lot. But I don't come with a price tag."

NEW ARRIVALS

The next morning there were indeed two fresh corpses on Professor Kern's dissecting table.

The two new heads designated for public demonstration were not supposed to know about the existence of Professor Dowell's head. That was why Professor Kern had it moved to the next room.

The male body belonged to a worker of about thirty years old who died in traffic. His powerful body was crushed. His half-open glassy eyes were filled with terror.

Professor Kern, Lauran and John dressed in white coats and were working on the bodies.

"There were several others," Professor Kern said. "One construction worker fell from the scaffolding. I rejected him. He could have had a concussion. I also rejected a few suicides who used poison. This guy seemed suitable. And this one... the night butterfly."

He nodded at the body of a woman with an attractive but faded face. It still bore the traces of rouge and eye pencil. The face was calm. Only the slightly raised eyebrows and half-open mouth expressed a kind of childish surprise.

"She's a nightclub singer. Was killed by a stray bullet during a fight between some drunk scoundrels. Straight through the heart, see? You couldn't make that shot on purpose, even if you wanted to."

Professor Kern worked quickly and confidently. The heads were separated from the bodies, and the bodies – taken away.

In a few more minutes the heads were set atop tall glass tables. Tubes were inserted into their throats, veins and arteries.

Professor Kern was in a state of pleasant excitement. The time of his triumph approached. He had no doubt in his success.

All the greatest scientific minds were invited to Professor Kern's upcoming demonstration and lecture. The press, guided by a skilled hand, published preliminary articles, in which Kern's scientific genius was being celebrated. Magazines posted his portraits. Kern's approaching performance was being treated as one of the triumphs of national science.

Whistling merrily, Professor Kern washed his hands, lit a cigar and watched the heads in front of him.

"Hehe! Not only was it John's head that ended up on a platter, but Salome's as well. That would have been some meeting, no? All we need to do is open the valve and... the dead shall come back to life. Well, Mademoiselle? Go ahead, revive them. Open all three valves. This big reservoir contains pressurized air, not poison, hehe..."

Of course, that was no longer news to Loran. But she habitually pretended to be surprised.

Kern frowned, suddenly serious. He came up to Lauran and said with utmost clarity, "I would like to ask you to not use Professor Dowell's air valve. His... vocal cords are... damaged and..."

34

Catching Lauran's doubtful gaze he added in irritation, "Regardless of the reason, I forbid you to open it. Please do as you are told, unless you want to get into serious trouble."

Returning to his happy mood, he sang the first line from the opera *Pagliacci*, "And so, we begin!"

Lauran opened the valves.

The worker's head was the first to show signs of life. His eyelids twitched slightly. His pupils became transparent.

"We have circulation. All is going well..."

Suddenly, the head's eyes changed their direction and looked at the window. The consciousness was slowly returning.

"He's alive!" Kern shouted happily. "Turn up the air stream."

Lauran opened the valve further.

Air whistled through the head's throat.

"What is this? Where am I?" the head mumbled.

"You are in a hospital, my friend," Kern said.

"A hospital?" the head moved its eyes, lowered them and saw the empty space underneath.

"Where are my legs? My arms? Where is my body?"

"It's gone, my dear man. It's been shattered to bits. The head was the only thing left, but the body had to be cut away."

"What do you mean cut away? No, I disagree. What kind of surgery is that? What am I good for? I can't earn a living with just my head. I need hands. Who will hire me without arms and legs? When I check out from the hospital... Damn! I can't even walk out of here. What am I to do? I have to eat and drink. I know how our hospitals are. You'll keep me here for a bit and then kick me out. No, I object."

His accent, his broad, suntanned, freckled face, his hair, and the naïve gaze of his blue eyes betrayed a country boy. Poverty drove him away from his native fields and the city tore apart his strong young body.

"Perhaps, I can get some kind of pension? And what about the other?" he suddenly remembered and his eyes widened.

"Who?"

"That guy… who ran me over… There was a tram, and another one, and that car that went straight at me."

"Don't worry. He shall get his due. The license plate of the truck has been recorded: four-seven-one-one, if you want to know. What is your name?" Professor Kern asked.

"Me? Tomas. Tomas Bouche, that was my name."

"Very well, Tomas. You shall want for nothing and you need not worry about being hungry, or thirsty, or cold. Nobody will throw you out into the street, you need not worry."

"So, are you just going to keep me for free or are you going to show me at the circus for money?"

"We will indeed show you, but not at the circus. We shall show you to scientists. And now you must rest. " Glancing at the woman's head, Kern noted anxiously, "Salome is running late."

"Is that another head without a body?" Tomas' head asked.

"As you see, we invited a lady so that you wouldn't get bored. Mademoiselle Lauran, close his air valve, please, to keep him from talking too much."

Kern pulled the thermometer from the woman's nose.

"The temperature is above that of a corpse, but still low. The revitalization is going slowly."

Time passed. The woman's head still did not come to life. Professor Kern became concerned. He walked around the laboratory, checked the clock, and his every step reverberated through the large room.

Tomas' head watched him in confusion and silently moved its lips.

Finally Kern approached the woman's head and carefully examined the glass tubes that topped the rubber pipes inserted into the arteries.

"Here is the problem. This tube is too small, and the circulation is slow. Give me a larger tube."

Kern replaced the glass tip and the head came to life in a few minutes.

Briquet's head – that was the woman's name – reacted to her revival much more emotionally. When she regained consciousness and started talking, she started shouting hoarsely, begging to be killed rather than be left so disfigured.

"Ah, ah, ah! My body, my poor body! What did you do with it? Either save me or kill me. I cannot live without a body! Let me look at it, or no... no... don't. It has no head... that is terrible! Terrible!"

When she calmed down a bit, she said, "You say you brought me back to life. I am not well-educated, but I know that a head cannot live without a body. Is this magic or sorcery?"

"Neither. It's a scientific achievement."

"If your science is capable of such miracles, then it ought to be able to do other things. Give me another body. Stupid George put a hole through me. But how many girls shoot themselves in the head over a man? Cut off one of their bodies and sew my head onto it. But show it to me first. I must have a beautiful body. But this is impossible... A woman without a body is worse than a man without a head."

She asked Lauran, "Would you be so kind as to give me a mirror."

Looking in the mirror, Briquet studied herself carefully and seriously.

"Awful! Would you please fix my hair? I can't even do my own hair..."

"You shall have more work, Mademoiselle Lauran," Kern chuckled. "Your compensation shall increase accordingly. I must go."

He glanced at the watch and whispered to Lauran, "In their presence," and he pointed at the heads with his eyes, "not a word must be spoken about Professor Dowell's head!"

When Kern left the laboratory, Lauran went to visit Professor Dowell.

Dowell's eyes gazed at her sadly. A sarcastic smile twisted his lips.

"My poor, poor professor..." Lauran whispered. "Soon, you shall be avenged!"

The head signed to her. Lauran opened the air valve.

"I'd rather have you tell me about today's experiment," the head hissed with a weak grin.

ENTERTAINING THE HEADS

The heads of Tomas and Briquet had an even harder time adjusting to their new existence than Dowell's head. The professor's brain could still work on the same scientific problems that interested him in the past. But Tomas and Briquet were simple people, and their life had no meaning without a body. It was no wonder that they soon became depressed.

"Is this life?" Tomas complained. "I am stuck here like a tree stump. I think I've stared a hole through that wall by now."

Kern was very concerned by the low spirits of the "prisoners of science" as he jokingly called them. The heads might waste away from melancholy before their demonstration.

And Professor Kern attempted to entertain them.

He bought a projector, and Lauran worked with John to arrange movie nights, using the white wall of the laboratory as their screen.

Tomas' head particularly enjoyed comedies with Charlie Chaplin and Monty Banks. When he watched their antics, Tomas forgot about his miserable existence for a time. Something like laughter burst forth from his throat and there were tears in his eyes.

But one time, after Banks has completed his performance, a farm appeared on the white wall of the room. A little girl was feeding chickens. A hen was attending to its babies. Next to a barn, a young healthy woman was milking a cow, pushing aside a

40

calf, who kept trying to stick its face under the udder. A furry dog ran up, happily wagging its tail, followed by a farmer. He was leading a horse by the reins.

Tomas wheezed in an uncommonly high unnatural voice and suddenly screamed, "No! Don't!"

John, who was working with the projector did not understand right away what was wrong.

"Stop the film!" Lauran shouted and quickly turned on the lights. Pale images flickered for a few more seconds and finally vanished when John stopped the projector.

Lauran looked at Tomas. There were tears in his eyes, but they were not from laughter. His entire plump face was twisted in a grimace, like that of an upset child, and his mouth was crooked, "Just like... our village..." he said, crying. "A cow, a hen... It's gone, it's all gone now."

Lauran went back to the projector. Soon, the lights were off again and shadows flickered on the white wall. Harold Lloyd was running away from the police. But Tomas' mood was ruined. The sight of moving people made him even more depressed.

"Look at him running around back and forth," Tomas head grumbled. "If he was stuck here, he wouldn't be running all over the place."

Lauran tried changing the program once again.

The sight of a society ball had completely upset Briquet. Beautiful women in their gorgeous gowns irritated her.

"Don't... I don't want to see how other people live," she said.

The projector had to be put away.

The radio kept them entertained somewhat longer.

They were both moved by the music, especially the dance tunes.

"My God, how I used to dance to this piece!" Briquet exclaimed once, bursting into tears.

They had to find other ways to entertain the heads.

Briquet was fussy, demanded a mirror every minute, invented new hairdos, asked to line her eyes with the eye pencil, powder and rouge her face. She was irritated by Lauran's lack of skill and her inability to comprehend the mysteries of makeup.

"Can't you see," Briquet's head said in frustration, "that the right eye is lined darker than the left. Raise the mirror higher."

She wanted to have fashion magazines and bolts of cloth to drape over her table.

She went so far as to state, with belated modesty, that she could not sleep in the same room with a man.

"Please shield me during the night with a screen, or at least with a book."

Lauran made a "screen" out of a large open book and started putting it on Briquet's table every night.

Tomas was also a handful.

One time he demanded wine. Professor Kern was forced to deliver the pleasure of inebriation by adding small doses of intoxicating substances into his feeding solutions.

Sometimes Tomas and Briquet sang together. Their weakened vocal cords were difficult to control, which made for a terrible duet.

"My poor voice... If only you could have heard me sing before!" Briquet said and her eyebrows rose sadly.

In the evenings they tended to be pensive. The strange nature of their existence forced even these simple characters think about the questions of life and death.

Briquet believed in life after death. Tomas was a materialist.

"Of course we are immortal," Briquet's head said. "If our soul died with the body, it could have never come back into the head."

"But where was your soul, in your head or in your body?" Tomas asked mockingly.

"Of course it was in the body... everywhere..." Briquet's head replied hesitantly, suspecting a trap.

"Does that mean that your soul is wandering headless around heaven?"

"You are the one that's headless." Briquet was offended.

"No, I've still got my head. That's the only thing I've got," Tomas wouldn't give up. "But your head's soul refused to stay up there. It came back down this rubber tube. No," he said seriously, "we are like machines. Turn on the steam – and we work. But if we shatter to pieces, there is no steam in the world to put us back together again."

And each one went back to his thoughts.

HEAVEN AND EARTH

Tomas' arguments did not convince Briquet. Despite her desultory way of life, she was a devout Catholic. While she was alive and too busy living, she didn't make time not only to think about life after death but even to go to church. But the religiosity she grew up with since she was a child was still firmly in place. Her present position provided a perfect soil for the seeds of this religiosity to spring to life. Her life as it was at the moment was terrible, but death – the possibility of second death – frightened her even more. At night she was tortured by the nightmares of the underworld.

She imagined the hellish flames. She saw her body being fried on an enormous pan.

Briquet woke up in terror, with her teeth chattering and her breath short. Yes, she most certainly felt as if she was suffocating. Her excited brain demanded additional oxygen, but she was deprived of a heart – that living engine that controlled so perfectly the blood supply to all of the organs. She tried shouting to wake up John who was on lab duty at night. But John became tired of frequent disruptions and, in order to get some sleep, he turned off the heads' air valves, despite Professor Kern's demands. Briquet opened her mouth like a fish out of water, and tried to scream, but made no sound. The room seemed to be filled with black chimaera shadows, hellfire lighting their terrible faces. They approached her and reached their clawed hands toward her.

44

Briquet closed her eyes, but it didn't help; she continued seeing them. The strange thing was that her heart seemed to pause and grow cold in horror.

"My God, my God, won't you forgive your slave, for you are omnipotent," her lips moved silently, "and your kindness is boundless. I have sinned much, but was that my fault? You know how it happened. I do not remember my mother; there was no one to teach me how to be good. I was starving. How many times have I asked you to come to my aid. Do not be angry, God, I am not reproaching you," she fearfully continued her silent prayer, "I am just trying to say that I am not that guilty. Perhaps, in your mercy, you can send me to purgatory. But not to hell! I shall die of terror... How stupid, you can't die once you are there!" and she began her naïve prayers once again.

Tomas slept badly too. But he was not tormented by horrors of hell. He was consumed by the longing for earthly things. Only a few months earlier he left his native village, leaving behind everything that was dear to him, taking only a small sack with some pies and his dreams – to earn enough money to buy a scrap of land. Then he could marry the pink-cheeked Marie, because her father wouldn't mind.

And then everything came crashing down. On the white wall of his unexpected prison he saw a farm and a happy young woman that looked so much like Marie, milking a cow. But instead of him, Tomas, some other man led a horse across the yard past the hen and chicks. And he, Tomas, was killed and demolished, and his

45

head has been stuck on a stick like a scarecrow. Where were his strong hands and his healthy body? Tomas gnashed his teeth in desperation. Then he cried quietly and tears fell onto the glass table.

"What is this?" Lauran asked in surprise during the morning cleanup. "Where did this water come from?"

While the air valves had been turned back on by John, Tomas said nothing. He gazed at Lauran glumly and unkindly, and when she stepped over to attend to Briquet's head, he quietly wheezed, "Murderer!" He had forgotten about the driver who ran him over and transferred all his anger upon people around him.

"What did you say, Tomas?" Lauran turned to him. But Tomas' lips were firmly pressed together once again, and his eyes stared at her with unbidden fury.

Lauran was surprised and wanted to ask John about the reasons for Tomas' bad mood, but Briquet had already taken over.

"Be so kind as to scratch the right side of my nose. This helplessness is terrible. Is there a pimple there? But then why is it so itchy? Bring me the mirror please."

Lauran put the mirror near Briquet's head.

"Turn it to the right, I can't see. More... Yes. There is some redness there. Perhaps we should try cold cream."

Lauran patiently applied the cream.

"Very nice. Some powder. Thank you. Mademoiselle Lauran, I wanted to ask you something."

"Of course."

"Tell me… If a great sinner confesses to a priest and admits to all her sins, can that person be absolved and go to heaven?"

"Of course she can," Lauran replied seriously.

"I am so afraid of torture in hell…" Briquet admitted. "Please, may I see a priest? I wish to die a true Christian."

And Briquet rolled her eyes up like a dying martyr. Then she lowered them and exclaimed, "I love the cut of your dress! Is this the latest fashion? It's been a long time since you brought me fashion magazines."

Briquet's thoughts quickly returned to more material subjects.

"A short hem… Good legs look great in short skirts. My legs! My poor legs! Have you seen them? Oh, when I danced, these legs drove men mad!"

Professor Kern entered the room.

"How is it going?" he asked merrily.

"Listen, Monsieur Professor," Briquet addressed him, "I cannot live like this. You must give me someone's body. I have already asked you, and I am asking you again. Please. I am certain that you could do that if you really wanted to."

"Damn it, why not?" Professor Kern thought. While he entirely appropriated all of the credit of reviving a human head separated from the body, he knew that its success was entirely due to Professor Dowell. But why not go beyond Dowell? Make one living person out of two dead ones – it would be tremendous! And if the experiment was successful, all the credit would belong to Kern alone. Although, he would still have to use some advice from Dowell's head. Yes, it was definitely worth considering.

"Do you want to dance some more?" Kern smiled and blew a stream of cigarette smoke into Briquet's face.

"Do I ever? I shall dance day and night. I shall swing my arms like a windmill and flutter about like a butterfly. Just give me a body – a young beautiful female body!"

"Why female?" Kern asked playfully. "If you wish, I could give you a male body."

Briquet looked at him with surprise and horror.

"A man's body? A woman's head on a man's body! No, no, that would be terrible! I can't even think of an appropriate outfit."

"But you won't be a woman anymore. You shall turn into a man. You shall grow a beard and moustache, and your voice will change too. Don't you want to turn into a man? Many women regret not being born a man."

"They must be women who men don't pay attention to. They, of course, would benefit from turning into a man. But I... I have no need." And Briquet proudly raised her lovely eyebrows.

"Very well, then. You shall remain a woman. I'll try to find you a suitable body."

"Oh, Professor, I shall be eternally grateful to you. Can we do it today? I can imagine the effect I shall have when I return to *Chat Noir*!"

"This is not something that can be done quickly."

Briquet continued chattering away, but Kern had already stepped away and was talking to Tomas.

"How are you doing, my friend?"

Tomas did not hear professor's talk to Briquet. Occupied by his thoughts, he glumly looked at Kern and said nothing.

Ever since Professor Kern promised Briquet a new body, her mood took a turn. Nightmares of hell no longer hounded her. She no longer thought about life after that. All her thoughts were consumed by the cares of her new earthly life. When she looked in the mirror, she worried that her face became thinner and her skin had a yellowish tinge. She has been wearing out Lauran, demanding to have her hair curled and her makeup applied.

"Professor, will I really remained so thin and yellow?" she asked Kern anxiously.

"You'll be prettier than ever," he assured her.

"I see that makeup is not sufficient, it's nothing but self-deception," she said when the professor left. "Mademoiselle Lauran, we shall do cold baths and massage. I have new wrinkles at my eyes and from my nose to my lips. I think they would go away if we massage them. A friend of mine… Ah, yes, I forgot to ask you, did you find some gray silk for my dress? Gray has always been my best color. Have you brought fashion magazines? Excellent! It's a pity that I do not know my size. I don't know what my body will be like. It would be nice if he could find something tall, with narrow hips. Open the magazine, please."

49

And she became immersed into the mysteries of women's outfits.

Lauran did not forget about Professor Dowell's head. She still took care of it and worked with it during morning hours, but there was no time to talk. Lauran still had much to discuss with Dowell. She was still tired and nervous. Briquet's head gave her not a moment of peace. Sometimes Lauran had to set aside her reading and run to Briquet's call only to fix a strand of hair or tell her about the underwear shop.

"But you still don't know the size of your new body," Lauran said, trying to contain her irritation, fixed Briquet's hair and rushed back to Dowell.

The thought of the bold surgery captivated Kern.

He worked tirelessly, preparing for the complex operation. He locked himself in with Professor Dowell's head and talked to it. Much as he wanted to, Kern could not do without Dowell's advice. Dowell pointed out an entire range of complications that Kern did not think about and that could be detrimental to the outcome of the experiment, and advised to carry out several preliminary experiments with animals. He also oversaw these experiments. And – such was the power of Dowell's intellect – he too became extremely engaged in the upcoming surgery. Dowell's head even looked younger. His thought was working with surpassing clarity.

Kern was both pleased and disgruntled by such extensive help from Dowell. The further the work continued, the more Kern realized that he could have never handled it without Dowell. All he

50

could do was indulge his vanity by the notion that he would be the one to bring these ideas to life.

"You are a worthy successor to the late Professor Dowell," Dowell's head said to him once with a barely noticeable ironic smile. "Ah, if only I could take a more active part in this work!"

This was neither a request nor a hint. Dowell's head knew all too well that Kern wouldn't want to give it a new body.

Kern frowned but pretended that he did not hear the exclamation.

"Well then, the experiments with animals went well," he said. "I operated two dogs. I decapitated them, and attached their heads to each other's bodies. They are both well and the stitches are healing fast."

"Feeding?" the head asked.

"Artificial for now. I only give them the antiseptic iodine solution through the mouth. But soon they should be able to eat normally."

In a few days, Kern announced, "The dogs are eating normally. The bandages have been taken off, and I think they should be able to run around in a day or two."

"Wait a week," the head advised. "Young dogs tend to make abrupt movements with their heads, and the stitches might come apart. Don't force it." The head wanted to add, "You'll have time to enjoy your laurels," but held back. "One more thing: keep the dogs in separate crates. They might get into a scuffle and hurt one another."

51

Finally, Professor Kern brought into Dowell's room a dog with a black head and a white body. The dog was clearly feeling well. Its eyes were bright and it happily wagged its tail. When it saw Professor Dowell's head, the dog's hair suddenly stood on end, it growled and barked in an odd wild voice. The strange sight must have shocked and frightened it.

"Take the dog around the room," the head said.

Kern walked around the room with the dog on a leash. Nothing slipped from Dowell's trained eye.

"What is that?" Dowell asked. "The dog is limping slightly on its hind left leg. And the voice seems to be off."

Kern looked taken aback.

"The dog limped prior to the surgery," he said, "its leg was broken before."

"I cannot see the defect and, alas, I cannot verify it by touch. Could you not have found a pair of healthy dogs?" the head asked doubtfully. "I think you can be completely sincere with me, my dear colleague. You must have taken too long when reviving them and prolonged the 'death pause' in heartbeat and breathing. As you know very well from my own experiments, this often leads to the disruption of the nervous system functions. Don't worry, such things may eventually go away. Just make sure your Briquet doesn't limp with both legs."

Kern was enraged but tried not to show it. The head had all the qualities of the former Professor Dowell – direct, demanding, and self-assured.

"This is outrageous!" Kern thought. "This head, hissing like a punctured tire, continues to lecture to me and make fun of my mistakes, and I have to listen to it like a schoolboy. One turn of a valve and I could be rid of this rotten pumpkin." Instead, Kern did his best not to betray his mood and listened carefully to a few more pieces of advice.

"Thank you for your instruction," Kern said, nodded and left.

Once he was behind the door he once again felt better.

"No," Kern consoled himself, "it was excellent work. Dowell is hard to please. The dog's limping and odd voice are nothing compared to what's been done."

When he passed through the room where Tomas and Briquet were situated, he stopped and said, pointing at the dog, "Mademoiselle Briquet, your wish will soon come true. See this dog? It used to be a head without a body, just like you, and look at it now. It lives and runs around as if nothing happened."

"I am not a dog," Briquet's head replied defensively.

"But it was a necessary experiment. If the dog could come to life in its new body, then so could you."

"I don't understand what the dog has to do with it," Briquet repeated stubbornly. "I don't care about the dog. I'd rather have you tell me when I shall be revived. Instead of taking care of me, you are wasting your time with dogs."

Kern gave up and said, continuing to smile, "Soon. We just need to find a suitable corpse… or a body, and you shall be back in shape, so to say."

53

Having taken the dog back to its pen, Kern returned with a measuring tape in his hands and carefully measured the circumference of Briquet's neck.

"Fourteen and a quarter inches," he said.

"My God, have I really grown that thin?" Briquet's head exclaimed. "It used to be fifteen. And my shoe size…"

Kern ignored her and quickly went to his study. As soon as he settled down at his desk, there was a knock on his door.

"Come in."

The door opened and Lauran entered. She did her best to remain calm, but her face was anxious.

VICE AND VIRTUE

"What is the matter? Is something wrong with the heads?" Kern asked looking up from his papers.

"No, but I wanted to speak with you, Professor."

Kern leaned back in his armchair.

"I am listening, Mademoiselle Lauran."

"Tell me, are you seriously intending to give Briquet a new body, or are you just trying to keep her calm?"

"I am absolutely serious."

"And you have reasons to believe that the surgery will be successful?"

"Entirely. You have seen the dog."

"Do you intend to put Tomas… back on his feet?" Lauran didn't dare approach her real question directly.

"Why not? He had asked about it. But I can't take care of everyone at once."

"What about Dowell?" Lauran started speaking quickly and anxiously. "Of course, everyone has the right to live a normal human life, including Tomas and Briquet. But you must understand that Dowell's value is higher than the rest. If you want to bring Tomas and Briquet back to life, it is so much more important to do the same for Professor Dowell."

Kern frowned. His entire face turned harsh and cautious.

"Professor Dowell, or rather his professorial head, found a wonderful defender in you," he said, smiling sarcastically. "But there is no need to defend him, and you need not be so upset and anxious. Of course I have thought about reviving Dowell's head as well."

"Then why don't you begin the experiment with him?"

"For the very reason that Dowell's head is more valuable than a thousand other heads. I began with the dog before giving a body to Briquet. Briquet's head is as many times more valuable than a dog as Dowell's head is more valuable than Briquet's."

"A human life and that of a dog are incomparable, Professor."

"Nor are the heads of Dowell and Briquet. Do you have anything else to say?"

"Nothing, Professor," Lauran replied and went to the door.

"In that case, Mademoiselle, I have a few questions for you. Please, wait."

Lauran halted by the door and looked at Kern questioningly.

"Please, come back to the desk and sit down."

Lauran settled back into the deep armchair feeling vaguely uneasy. Kern's face promised nothing good. Kern leaned back in his chair and stared at length into Lauran's eyes, as if searching for something, until she looked down. He then rose to his formidable height, planted his fists firmly on the desk, leaned toward Lauran and asked her quietly and imposingly, "Tell me, did you turn on Dowell's air valve? Did you talk to him?"

Lauran felt the tips of her fingers grow cold. Thoughts whirled through her head. Her anger against Kern was boiling and ready to burst free.

"Should I or should I not tell the truth?" Lauran hesitated. Oh, how much she would have enjoyed throwing the word "murderer" into this man's face, but such open attack could ruin everything.

Lauran did not believe that Kern would give Dowell's head a new body. She knew enough to trust such possibility. All she could dream of was to strip Kern of his crown acquired by taking credit for Dowell's work, to do so publicly and uncover his crimes. She knew that nothing would stop Kern and declaring herself as his enemy; she subjected her life to danger. It wasn't the sense of self-preservation that stopped her. She did not want to perish before Kern's crimes were made public. And in order to do that, she had to lie. But her conscience and all of her upbringing revolted against lying. She had never had to lie in her life and was now in a state of turmoil.

Kern never took his eyes off her face.

"Don't lie," he said mockingly, "don't burden your conscience with that sin. You have been talking to the head, don't deny it, because I already know. John has been listening in."

Lauran kept looking down and remained silent.

"I am just curious to know what you talked about."

Lauran felt blood rush to her face. She looked up and looked Kern in the eyes.

"About everything."

"Right," Kern said, still leaning on his desk. "That's what I thought. About everything."

He paused. Lauran lowered her eyes once again and looked like a person waiting for a sentence.

Kern suddenly went to the door and locked it. He paced several time across the soft carpet of his study, his hands behind his back. He then quietly walked up to Lauran and asked, "Then what do you plan to do, dear girl? Turn the terrible monster Kern over to the judges? Drag his name through mud? Uncover his crimes? Did Dowell ask you about that?"

"No, no," forgetting her fear, Lauran said passionately, "I assure you that Professor Dowell is completely devoid of the sense of revenge. Oh, his is a noble soul! He even tried to... talk me out of it. He is not like you, you can't judge everyone based on yourself!" she finished, her eyes flashing.

Kern chuckled and once again paced around his study.

"Very well, excellent. Then you did have intentions of going public, and had it not been for Dowell's head, Professor Kern would have been in prison. If virtue cannot triumph, then at least vice must be punished. Such is the ending of all the well-intentioned novels you have ever read, is it not, dear girl?"

"And vice shall be punished!" she exclaimed, nearly losing control of her emotions.

"Oh, of course, up there in heaven." Kern looked up at the ceiling with its large squares of black oak. "But here on earth, as you might not know, you naïve creature, vice is the one to triumph, and only vice! And virtue... Virtue stands there with its hand held out, begging vice for pennies, or sits over there," Kern pointed

58

toward the room where he kept Dowell's head, "like a scarecrow, pondering the burdens of human existence."

He came up to Lauran, lowered his voice and said, "Do you know, I can literally turn you and Dowell's head to ashes, and not a single soul will know."

"I know you are capable of any…"

"Crime? It is very well that you know."

Kern once again walked around the room and continued talking in his regular voice, as if thinking out loud, "But what do you wish me to do, my beautiful avenger? Unfortunately, you are the kind of person who will not stop before anything and are prepared to accept martyrdom for the sake of truth. You are fragile, nervous, impressionable; but you are not easily intimidated. Must I kill you? Today, right this moment? I can cover up the tracks but it would still be messy. And my time is valuable. Must I bribe you? It's even more difficult than trying to scare you. Well, tell me, what am I to do with you?"

"Leave everything as it was. After all, I haven't reported you yet."

"And will you report me in the future?"

Lauran considered her answer, then replied quietly and firmly, "I will."

Kern stomped his foot.

"Ah, you stubborn girl! Here is what I'll do. Sit down at the desk. Don't worry, I am not going to strangle or poison you yet. Sit."

Lauran looked at him in puzzlement, thought about it and moved to the chair at the desk.

"Unfortunately, I have use for you. If I kill you now, I shall have to find a replacement. And there is no guarantee that your successor won't turn out to be some sort of blackmailer who discovers Dowell's head and then starts sucking money out of me, and then report me anyway. At least I know you. So, write this, 'Dearest mommy,' or whatever else you call your mother, 'the condition of patients I take care of requires my constant presence at Professor Kern's house'."

"You wish to take away my freedom? Imprison me in your house?" Lauran asked indignantly.

"Exactly so, my virtuous assistant."

"I refuse to write such a letter," Lauran stated firmly.

"Enough!" Kern suddenly shouted so loudly that the spring in the clock hummed. "Understand, I have no other choice. Don't be an idiot."

"I will not stay here and I will not write the letter!"

"Indeed! Very well. You may go wherever you please. But before you leave, you shall watch as I take the life of Dowell's head and dissolve it in a chemical solution. Then you may go and scream out loud to the entire world that you had seen Dowell's head. No one shall believe you. People will laugh at you. But beware! Your accusations will not remain without revenge. Come!"

Kern grabbed Lauran's hand and pulled her to the door. She was too weak to resist his brutishness.

Kern unlocked the door, quickly passed through Tomas' and Briquet's room and entered the room where Professor Dowell's head was being kept.

Dowell's head watched this unexpected visit in puzzlement. Without paying any attention to it, Kern quickly walked up to the array of devices and turned down the valve on the blood supply cylinder.

The head's eyes, confused, but calm, looked at the valve, then at Kern and then at the dismayed Lauran. The air valve was closed and the head could not speak. It moved its lips and Lauran, who was used to the head's expressions by now, realized that it was the silent question, "The end?"

Then the head's eyes started fading, the eyelids opened wide, the eyeballs bulged and the face started twitching. The head was going through the torture of suffocation.

Lauran screamed. She then walked up to Kern, grabbed his arm and, almost fainting, said in a halting voice, "Open, open the valve. I'll do anything!"

With a barely noticeable grin, Kern opened the valve. The liquid flowed down the tube toward Dowell's head. Its face stopped twitching, its eyes assumed a normal expression and its gaze cleared. Life returned to Dowell's head, having been nearly snuffed out. His consciousness remained as well, because Dowell once again looked at Lauran with the expression of confusion and partial disappointment.

Lauran was unsteady on her feet.

"May I offer you my arm," Kern said gallantly, and the odd couple walked out.

Once Lauran was settled at the deck, Kern said as if nothing happened, "Where were we? Right. 'The condition of the patients requires my constant,' or rather, 'my uninterrupted presence at Professor Kern's house. Professor Kern was so kind as to provide me with a beautiful room with the view of his garden. In addition, because my workday has become longer, Professor Kern has tripled my salary'."

Lauran looked at Kern reproachfully.

"It's true," he said. "Necessity forces me to deprive you of your freedom, but I must compensate you somehow. I really am increasing your salary. Continue, 'Service here is wonderful, and while I have a lot of work, I feel great. Don't come to see me, the professor does not receive anyone. But don't worry, I shall write often.' Right. Now add some sweet nonsense you would normally write to avoid any suspicion."

As if forgetting about Lauran, Kern continued to think out loud, "Of course, this cannot continue. But I hope I shall not have to detain you for long. Our work is approaching the end and then... That is, I mean the head hasn't got long. Soon it will be no more. Why do I bother, you know what I mean. To make a long story short, when Dowell and I finish our work, Dowell will be finished as well. There won't be even a speck of ash left from the head, and then you may return to your respected mama. You shall have no danger to me. Once again: keep in mind, if you dare talk, I have witnesses who are prepared to swear under oath that Professor Dowell's remains, including his head and other bits of his professorial body, were cremated by me after the autopsy. Crematorium is a very convenient thing for just such cases."

Kern rang the bell. John came in.

John, you shall take Mademoiselle Lauran to the white room with the garden window. Mademoiselle Lauran is moving in with us, because we have a lot of work ahead. Ask Mademoiselle whether she needs anything to be comfortable and get her everything she wants. You may place orders at any shops over the phone and charge them to my name. I shall pay all the bills. Do not forget to order supper for Mademoiselle."

Kern bowed and left.

John took Lauran to her room.

Kern didn't lie – the room was truly lovely. It was spacious, bright and well-furnished. An enormous window looked out into the garden. But even the grimmest prison could not have made Lauran more depressed than this pretty, cheerful room. Feeling almost physically ill, Lauran made it to the window and glanced out.

"Second floor. Too high to run away," she thought. Even if she could run away, she would not have, because doing so would have been equivalent to a death sentence for Dowell's head.

Lauran dropped onto the bed in exhaustion and went deep into thought. She could not tell how long she was in that state.

"Supper is served," she heard John's voice as if in a dream and looked up tiredly.

"Thank you, but I am not hungry. Please take it away."

The well-trained servant did as he was told and left.

She went back to her thoughts. When lights came on in the windows of the building across, she felt so lonely that she went to see the heads. She particularly wanted to see Dowell.

Lauran's sudden visit made Briquet very happy.

"Finally!' she exclaimed. "Already? Is it here?"

"What is?"

"My body," Briquet said as if she was talking about a new dress.

"No, not yet," Lauran replied, smiling despite herself. "But soon. You don't have long to wait."

"Ah, it couldn't be soon enough!"

"Will I get another body too?" Tomas asked.

"Yes, of course," Lauran reassured him. "And you shall be as healthy and strong as before. You shall earn enough money, go back home and marry your Marie."

Tomas smacked his lips.

"If only."

Lauran rushed to Dowell's room.

As soon as she turned on the air valve, the head asked her, "What was that all about?"

Lauran told the head about her conversation with Kern and her imprisonment.

"This is outrageous!" the head said. "If only I could help you. I could, if you help me."

The head's eyes were filled with anger and determination.

"It's very simple. Shut off the feeding tubes and I shall die. Trust me, I was even disappointed when Kern opened the valve and revived me. I shall die, and Kern will let you go home."

"I could never go home at such a price!" Lauran exclaimed.

"I wish I had all of Cicero's eloquence to convince you."

Lauran shook her head.

"Even Cicero couldn't convince me. I would never end a human life."

"But am I really human?" the head said with a sad smile.

"Remember, you yourself quoted Descartes, 'I think. Therefore, I am'," Lauran replied.

"I suppose so. Here is something else I could do. I could stop helping Kern. He won't be able to torture me into submission again. And then he'll kill me himself."

"No, no, I beg you," Lauran came closer to the head. "Listen. Before, I could think of nothing but revenge. But now I think differently. If Kern manages to attach Briquet's head to another body and the surgery is successful, there is hope of bringing you back to life. If not by Kern, then by someone else."

"Unfortunately, this hope is very weak," Dowell replied. "I doubt even Kern is capable of it. He is a wicked and criminal man, as vain as a thousand Herostrates. But he is a talented surgeon and, I must say, the most capable of all my assistants. If he fails,

65

having had the advantage of my guidance, then no one can succeed. However, I don't think even he can carry out this unprecedented operation."

"But the dogs…"

"The dogs are different. Both dogs, alive and well, were on the same table before the heads were switched. It took place very quickly. And I think Kern only managed to revive one dog, otherwise he would have brought both to brag. A body can only be delivered several hours after death, when the processes of decay may have already started. You, as a medical student, may judge the complexity of the surgery itself. It's not the same as re-attaching a half-separated finger. One must tie together, sew together all the arteries, veins and, most importantly, the nerves and the spinal column, otherwise you'll have a cripple; then you must restart circulation. No, it is an endlessly complex task, unconquerable even to the modern surgeons."

"Are you saying even you wouldn't have dared?"

"I have thought about everything, and I have done experiments with dogs so, I think, I may have pulled it off."

Suddenly the door opened. It was Kern.

"A council of conspirators? I won't stop you." And he slammed the door shut.

THE DEAD DIANA

Briquet's head seemed to think that to find and attach a new body to her head was as easy as to fit and sew a new dress. The neck circumference had been measured, and all that remained was to find a corpse with the same neck size.

However, she soon discovered that it wasn't that simple.

Professor Kern, Lauran and John came to see her in the morning, dressed in white coats. Kern directed his assistants to carefully take Briquet's head off the glass table and place it facing up to be able to see the entire section of the neck. The head continued to be fed with oxygen-saturated blood through the entire process. Kern focused on studying its anatomy and making critical measurements.

"While human anatomy is generally very uniform," Kern said, "every human body has its own peculiarities. Sometimes it is difficult to tell, for example, the exact position of the carotid artery. The thickness of the arteries is not always the same either, nor is the size of the windpipe, even for people with the same neck circumference. There is also much work to be done with the nerves."

"But then how are you going to operate?" Lauran asked. "Once you place the neck against the body, you shall cover up your entire working surface."

"Therein lies the problem. Dowell and I have been working on this issue. We shall have to make a series of lengthwise cuts —

going from the center to the outside. It is a very complex work. We shall have to make fresh cuts in the neck's head and in the neck of the corpse to get to the active living cells. But that is not the main complication. The main thing is to eliminate the products of decay or infection in the body, to clear the blood vessels from the coagulated blood, to fill them with fresh blood and to force the body's 'engine' – the heart to work again. And what about the spinal cord? The merest touch to it causes the most violent reaction, sometimes with very serious consequences."

"How do you plan to overcome these problems?"

"Oh, it is my secret for now. Once the experiment is successful, I shall publish the entire sequence of bringing someone back to life. Well, that's enough for today. Put the head back into place. Open the air valve. How do you feel, Mademoiselle?" Kern asked, addressing Briquet's head.

"Very well, thank you. But listen, Monsieur Professor, I am very concerned... You were talking about all kinds of unpleasant things, and one thing I did understand is that you are planning to slice and dice my neck all over. That will be terrible. How am I to go anywhere with the neck that looks like a pork chop?"

"I shall do my best to make the scars as subtle as possible. Of course, there will be no way to conceal the surgery entirely. Don't look at me so desperately, Mademoiselle, you can wear a velvet ribbon or even an entire necklace. Very well, I shall give you one on your 'birthday'. One other thing. Your head had dried up some. It is now smaller than it was when you were living a normal life.

So, in order to find out your normal neck size, we shall have to fatten you up a bit, otherwise there might be problems."

"But I can't eat," the head replied pitifully.

"We shall feed you through the tube. I prepared a special solution," he turned to Lauran. "We shall also have to increase the blood flow."

"Are you adding fats to the feeding solution?"

Kern made an indefinite gesture with his hand.

"Even if the head doesn't get fatter, it shall swell some, and that is exactly what we need. And so," he concluded, "all that is left is to pray to God, Mademoiselle Briquet, for some beauty to die and let you have her beautiful body after death."

"Don't say that, it's terrible! Someone must die in order for me to get a body... I am afraid, Doctor. It is going to be a dead body. What if her ghost comes back and demands its body back?"

"Her ghost?"

"Yes, the dead woman's ghost."

"But she won't have any legs to come to you," Kern replied, laughing. "And even if she does, then you shall tell her that you have given her body a head, instead of the other way around, and she should be grateful for the gift. I am off to keep watch at the morgue. Wish me luck!"

The success of the experiment largely depended on how fresh the corpse was going to be, which was why Kern abandoned all other matters and practically moved into the morgue to wait for his chance.

69

Cigar in his mouth, he paced around the long building as calmly as if he was taking a walk in the park. Subdued light fell upon the long rows of marble tables. On each table was a body, already washed and undressed.

Puffing on his cigar, with his hands in his pockets, Kern circled around the rows of table, looking at the faces, and from time to time raise the leather cover to examine a body.

He wasn't alone in his search. There were also friends and relatives of the dead. Kern was not too happy about them, afraid that they might snatch a suitable body away from him. Getting a corpse he needed wasn't that simple. Prior to the three-day deadline, any body could be claimed by relatives, and after the deadline, the half-decayed corpse would have no interest to Kern. He needed a completely fresh, preferably still-warm body.

Kern was generous with bribes to make certain he would get what he needed as quickly as possible. A body's number replaced and some unlucky girl could be recorded as "missing".

"It's not easy to find a goddess to suit Briquet's taste," Kern thought as he surveyed the broad feet and calloused hands of the corpses. Most of the people there were not of the kind that owned a car and a house. Kern went from one end of the hall to the other. During that time, several bodies had been identified and taken away, and the new ones were brought in. But even among the new arrivals Kern could not find anything suitable for the surgery. There were corpses without heads, but they were either of the wrong size, had body wounds or were already decaying.

The day was almost over. Kern felt hungry and fantasized with pleasure about chicken cutlets in a steaming pot.

"Bad day," Kern thought, pulling out his watch. He headed for the exit through the moving crowd of people filled with desperation, sadness and horror. The orderlies were carrying the body of a woman without a head. The freshly washed young body shone like white marble.

"Oh, this could be suitable," he thought and followed the orderlies. When the body was placed on a table, Kern examined it quickly and became convinced that he found what he was looking for. He already wanted to whisper to the orderlies to take the body away, when the body was approached by a badly-dressed old man with overgrown mustache and beard.

"Here she is. Martha!" he exclaimed and wiped his forehead.

"Damn him!" Kern cursed under his breath, walked up to the man and said, "You can identify the body? It has no head."

The old man pointed at a large mole on the left shoulder.

"This is how," he replied.

Kern was surprised by the old man's calm demeanor.

"Who was she? Your wife or daughter?"

"Neither, thank God," the talkative old man replied. "She was my cousin, once removed. My cousin died and left three of them for me to care for. I already had four of my own, and we aren't rich. But what was I to do, sir? They weren't kittens, I couldn't throw them in the dumpster. So, we got by. And then this happened. We live in an old house and were told to move, but

71

where were we to go? The roof collapsed, the other children only had bumps and bruises, but this one's head was cut clean off. My old lady and I were not home – we sell fried chestnuts. I came home, but Martha was already taken to the morgue. Why? They said people in other apartments were crushed too, and some of them had no family, so they were all brought here. I came home and couldn't get in, it was like an earthquake."

"This could work," Kern thought and, pulling the old man aside, said to him, "You can't fix what happened. You see, I am a doctor, and I need a body. I shall be honest. Would you like to go home with a hundred franks?"

"Are you going to cut her up?" the old man shook his head in disapproval and pondered. "Of course, she is gone anyway. We are poor people. And she is family."

"Two hundred."

"We are greatly in need, the kids are hungry… but still. She was a nice girl, very nice, very kind, the face like a rose, not like this trash…" the old man waved dismissively at the tables with other bodies.

"What a guy! I think he is beginning to advertise his merchandize," Kern thought and decided to change his strategy.

"As you wish," he said. "There are many bodies here, and some are no worse than your girl here," and Kern stepped away from the man.

"No, wait, let me think…" the old man shuffled after him, clearly considering the deal.

Kern was just about to celebrate, but the situation changed once again.

"There you are!" an anxious voice sounded.

Kern turned and saw a fat little old woman in a pristine white bonnet bearing down on them. The old man grunted at the sight of her.

"Have you found her?" the old woman asked, glancing around wildly and whispering prayers.

The old man silently pointed at the corpse.

"Our poor dove, you poor soul!" the old woman howled, coming closer to the headless body.

Kern saw that the lady would be more difficult to manage than her husband.

"Listen, Madam," he said kindly, addressing the old woman. "I was talking to your husband here, and found out that you are in great need."

"Whatever our need is, we don't take help from strangers," the woman said not without pride.

"Yes, but... you see, I am a member of a charitable funeral organization. I can organize your cousin's funeral and have all the expenses taken care of. If you wish, you can entrust me with the entire matter, and go home to your children and the orphans."

"What have you told him?" the old woman attacked her husband. She turned back to Kern and said, "Thank you, sir, but I must do everything properly. We shall manage somehow without your charitable organization. What are you rolling your eyes for?" she said to her husband. "Get going. I brought the cart."

It was said in such a decisive tone that Kern bowed and left.

"Damn! No, this is definitely not a good day."

He went to the exit and, pulling one of the orderlies off to the side, said quietly, "Keep an eye out, if there is anything suitable, call me immediately."

"Oh, absolutely, sir," the orderly nodded, having received a sizeable bribe from Kern.

Kern had a good dinner at a restaurant and went home.

When he entered Briquet's room, she met him with the only question she had been asking him lately, "Have you found it?"

"I have, but not quite, damn it!" he replied. "Be patient."

"Could you really not find anything suitable?" Briquet refused to give up.

"There were a few bandy-legged cuttlefish. If you wish, I could…"

"Oh no, I'd rather wait. I don't want to be bandy-legged."

Kern decided to go to bed earlier to get an early start the next morning to go to the morgue. But as soon as he fell asleep, his bedside phone rang. Kern cursed and picked up.

"Hello! Yes. Yes, this is Professor Kern. What? A train crash? Are there many bodies? Indeed! Of course, I shall be there immediately. Thank you."

Kern started dressing quickly, called John and shouted, "Get the car!"

74

In fifteen minutes he was already rushing through the night streets as if to a fire.

The orderly did not deceive him. Death had collected a large harvest that night. Bodies were being carried back and forth all over the place. All tables were occupied. Soon, bodies had to be left on the floor. Kern was delighted. He thanked the fates that the catastrophe did not take place during the day. Clearly, the news had not yet spread through the city. There were no other visitors at the morgue. Kern examined the corpses that weren't washed or undressed yet. They were all completely fresh. It was an exceptional chance. The only bad thing was that even this stroke of luck had no regard for Kern's special requirements. Most of the bodies were crushed or damaged all over. But Kern did not lose hope, because more bodies kept coming in.

"Show me this one," he addressed an orderly carrying a corpse of a young woman in a gray suit. Her skull was broken from the back. Her hair was covered in blood as were her clothes. But her suit was undamaged and unwrinkled. "Apparently, the damage to the body wasn't great. This will do. Her figure is somewhat plebeian – she must have been a maid or some such. But this body is better than none," Kern thought. "What about this?" Kern exclaimed and pointed at another stretcher. "What a find! A treasure! Damn it, it is sad that a woman like that had to die!"

The woman, whose body was lowered onto the floor, had an uncommonly beautiful aristocratic face bearing an expression of

75

deep surprise. Her skull was broken above the right ear. Apparently, she died instantaneously. There was a pearl necklace around her white neck. Her elegant black silk dress was only slightly torn at the bottom and from the neckline to the shoulder. There was a large mole on her shoulder.

"Like the other one," Kern thought. "But this… is so beautiful!" Kern quickly measured the neck, "Perfect!"

Kern pulled the necklace of real, large pearls off her neck, tossed it to the orderlies and said, "I take this body. But because I have no time to examine it more thoroughly, I shall take this one as well," and he pointed at the first body of the girl in gray. "Quick, quick. Wrap them in canvass and take them out. Do you hear that? A crowd is gathering. You will have to open the morgue and in a few minutes the whole place will be in a chaos."

The bodies were taken out, placed into his car and quickly delivered to Kern's house.

Everything needed for the surgery had long since been prepared. The day, or rather the night of Briquet's resurrection has come at last. Kern didn't want to lose a single moment.

Both corpses were washed, wrapped in sheets and placed on the operating table in Briquet's room.

Briquet's head couldn't wait to look at her new body, but Kern purposely positioned the table in such a way that she couldn't see the corpses until everything was ready.

Kern quickly cut off the heads. They were wrapped in canvas and taken out by John; the sections and the table were cleaned, and the bodies prepared.

Having thoroughly examined the bodies, Kern shook his head with concern. The body with the mole on the shoulder was flawlessly beautiful in its form and clearly superior compared to the body of the maid – big-boned, angular, imperfectly but strongly built. Of course, Briquet would choose the body of the aristocratic Diana. However, during his careful examination, Kern noticed a small defect in Diana's body, as he called her: there was a small scratch on the sole of the right foot, probably caused by a piece of metal. It did not present too much danger. Kern treated the scratch and disinfected it, there was no reason to worry about blood poisoning yet. Still, he would have felt more confident about the success of the surgery with the body of the maid.

"Turn Briquet's head," Kern said to Lauran. To keep Briquet from chattering during the preparation, her mouth was kept shut, that is her air valve was off. "You may turn the air on now."

When Briquet saw the corpses, she shrieked so loudly as if she was on fire. Her eyes widened in terror. One of these bodies was to become her own. For the first time she perceived the unusual nature of the surgery and hesitated.

"Well? How do you like these cor… these bodies?"

"I am… afraid…" the head wheezed. "No, no, I never thought it would be so terrible. I don't want to."

"No? I could attach one of them to Tomas' head. Tomas shall become a woman. Tomas, would you like to get a new body right away?"

"No, wait," Briquet's head exclaimed. "I agree. I want to have that one – the one with the mole on its shoulder."

"I would advise you to pick this one. It is not as handsome, but it hasn't got a single scratch."

"I am not a laundress, I am a performer," Briquet stated proudly. "I want to have a beautiful body. And the mole on the shoulder... Men really like that."

"Have it your way," Kern replied. "Mademoiselle Lauran, please transfer Mademoiselle Briquet's head onto the operating table. Do be careful, the artificial circulation must continue until the last moment."

Lauran worked on the last few things to prepare Briquet's head. Briquet's face was filled with strain and anxiety. When the head was transferred onto the table, Briquet couldn't stand it and suddenly screamed as she had never screamed before, "No! No! Don't! Kill me instead! I am scared! A-a-a-a-a!"

Without interrupting his work, Kern shouted at Lauran abruptly, "Shut down her air valve! Add the sedative to her feeding solution and she shall fall asleep."

"No, no, no!"

The valve was turned down, the head went mum, but continued moving its lips with a pleading and terrified look.

78

"Monsieur Professor, should we really go on with the surgery against her will?" Lauran asked.

"There is no time for these ethical problems right now," Kern replied dryly. "She'll thank us later. Do your job or leave and stay out of my way."

But Lauran knew that she could not leave – without her assistance, the outcome of the surgery would have been even more questionable. She overcame herself and continued helping Kern. Briquet's head thrashed so much that the tubes nearly came out of the blood vessels. John joined them and held the head in his hands. Gradually, the head stopped twitching, its eyes closed; the sedative was working.

Professor Kern continued with the surgery.

The silence was broken only by Kern's quick orders, asking for this or that surgical instrument. The strain was causing the veins on Kern's forehead to bulge. He used the full range of his spectacular surgical skills, combining speed with superior thoroughness and caution. Despite her hatred of Kern, Lauran could not help but admire him at that moment. He worked like an artist consumed by inspiration. His deft sensitive fingers were doing the impossible.

The surgery continued one hour and fifty-five minutes.

"It's over," Kern finally said, straightening, "Briquet is no longer a head without a body. All that is left is to breathe life into her: set her heart beating, restart her circulation. But that I can manage on my own. You may go rest, Mademoiselle Lauran."

"I can keep going," she replied.

Despite being tired, she very much wanted to see the last part of this unusual surgery. But Kern clearly didn't want to share the mystery of revival with her. He once again insisted that she must go rest and Lauran obeyed.

Kern called her back in an hour. He looked even more tired, but his face reflected deep satisfaction.

"Try the pulse," he offered Lauran.

Not without a shudder the girl took Briquet's hand, the very hand that belonged to a cold corpse only three hours prior. The hand was warm and there was the beating of the pulse. Kern held a mirror to Briquet's face. The surface became fogged.

"She is breathing. We must now wrap our newborn well. She must remain completely motionless for a few days."

In addition to the bandages, Kern put a cast around Briquet's neck. Her entire body was wrapped and her mouth covered.

"We can't have her talking," Kern explained. "During the first day we shall keep her sedated, as long as the heart allows."

Briquet was transferred to a room adjacent to Lauran's, carefully placed into bed and subject to electrical sedation.

"We shall feed her artificially, until the stitches heal. You shall have to take good care of her."

Only on the third day Kern allowed Briquet to regain consciousness.

It was four in the afternoon. A slanting sunbeam cut through the room and fell onto Briquet's face. She moved her eyebrows and opened her eyes. Still barely conscious, she looked at the sunlit window, then shifted her gaze at Lauran, then finally looked down. The space below was no longer empty. She saw the weakly moving chest and a body – her body, covered with a sheet. A weak smile lit her face.

"Do not try to talk and stay still," Lauran said. "The surgery went very well and now everything depends on how you behave yourself. The calmer you are, the sooner you shall be on your feet. In the meantime, we will communicate through signs. Lowering your eyelids means 'yes', raising them means 'no'. Does anything hurt? Here. Neck and foot. That shall pass. Are you thirsty? Hungry?" Briquet was not hungry but wanted something to drink.

Lauran called Kern. He immediately came over from his study.

"How does the newborn feel?" He examined her and remained pleased. "All is well. Patience, Mademoiselle, and you shall be dancing soon." He gave a few instructions and left.

The days of recovery went on very slowly for Briquet. She was a model patient: she restrained her impatience, lay still and followed all directions. Finally, she was unwrapped but was not yet allowed to talk.

"Can you feel your body?" Kern asked somewhat anxiously. Briquet lowered her eyelids.

"Please try to move your toes, very carefully."

Briquet was clearly trying, because her face reflected concentration and effort, but the toes didn't move.

81

"Apparently, the functions of the central nervous system are not yet fully restored," Kern said confidently. "But I hope they will be restored soon, and with them – the ability to move." To himself he thought, "I really do hope Briquet doesn't go limping with both feet."

"Restored – this word sounds so strange," Lauran thought as she remembered the cold corpse on the operating table.

Briquet made up a new task for herself. She spent hours trying to move her toes. Lauran watched her with great interest.

One day, Lauran exclaimed happily, "It moves! The left big toe is moving."

Things went faster after that. Other toes and fingers started moving as well. Soon Briquet could slightly lift her arms and legs.

Lauran was struck. A miracle was taking place before her very eyes.

"As criminal as Kern is," she thought, "he is a remarkable man. It is true that without Dowell's head he wouldn't have been able to perform this resurrection of the dead. But still, Kern is a talented man – Dowell's head said as much. Oh, if only Kern restored him as well! But no, he won't do it."

After a few days, Briquet was allowed to talk. She turned out to have a rather pleasant voice but of a somewhat broken timbre.

"It shall straighten out," Kern assured her. "You'll be able to sing.

Briquet did try to sing shortly. Lauran was greatly surprised by this singing. Briquet's high notes were rather squealy and not very pleasant, and in the middle range the voice sounded very dull and even hoarse. But the lower notes were charming. She had a splendid deep contralto.

"The vocal cords are above the cut and belong to Briquet," Lauran thought, "but then where is the double voice coming from, why the different tones in the upper and lower registers? It is a physiological mystery. I wonder if it is driven by the process of rejuvenation of Briquet's head, who was older than the new body? Or, perhaps, it was somehow related to the disruption of the functions of the central nervous system? It was unclear... I wonder, whose was this young graceful body?"

Without telling anything to Briquet, Lauran started checking the papers, which published the lists of people who died in the train crash. Soon, she stumbled onto an article saying that a famous Italian singer Angelica Gaye, who was traveling on that train, had vanished without a trace. Her body was never found, and newspaper reporters made up fantastic theories to solve this puzzle. Lauran was almost certain that Briquet's head received the body of the perished performer.

THE RUNAWAY EXHIBIT

Finally, the momentous day came. The last few of Briquet's bandages were taken off and Professor Kern allowed her to get up.

She rose and walked round the room, leaning on Lauran's arm. Her movements were uncertain and somewhat halting. Sometimes she made strange gestures with her arm; it moved smoothly up to a point, then there was a pause and a seemingly forced movement, and then it moved smoothly again.

"It will get better," Kern said confidently.

The only thing that worried him was the small scratch on Briquet's foot. It healed slowly. But eventually it too healed well enough for Briquet not to feel any pain when she walked. In a few more days, Briquet tried dancing.

"I don't understand what the matter is," she said. "Some movements come very easily to me, but the others are difficult. I suppose I am not yet used to using my new body. But it is splendid! Look at the legs, Mademoiselle Lauran. And the height is perfect. But these scars on my neck… I shall have to hide them. But the mole on the shoulder is charming, is it not? I shall have a dress made with a neckline to show it off. No, I am definitely pleased with my body."

"My body!" Lauran thought. "Poor Angelica Gaye!"

Everything Briquet held back for so long finally burst through all at once. She buried Lauran in requests, orders and shipments of clothes, underwear, shoes, hats, fashion magazines and makeup.

In a new gray silk dress she was introduced by Kern to Professor Dowell's head. Because it was a male head, Briquet couldn't help but flirt a little. She was very flattered, when Dowell's head wheezed, "Excellent! You have completed your task beautifully, colleague, congratulations!"

Kern left the room arm-in-arm with Briquet, beaming like a newlywed.

"Have a sit, Mademoiselle," Kern said gallantly, when they came to his study.

"I don't know how to thank you, Professor," she said, slowly lowering her eyes, then giving Kern a coquettish gaze. "You have done so much for me. But there is nothing I can do to reward you."

"There is no need. I am rewarded more than you can imagine."

"I am very glad." And Briquet bestowed another luminous gaze upon Kern. "But now I would like to leave, to check out from the hospital."

"What do you mean leave? What hospital?" Kern didn't even understand her at first.

"Go home. I can imagine the furor I shall cause among my friends!"

She wanted to leave! Kern didn't even want to think about it. He had done a tremendous amount of work, solved the most complicated problem, and did the impossible. He didn't do it all for the purpose of Briquet's causing a furor among her dim-witted friends. He himself wanted to cause a furor by showing Briquet to the scientific society. Subsequently, he might allow her greater freedom, but it would be impossible at the moment.

"Unfortunately, I cannot let you go, Mademoiselle Briquet. You must remain at my house for a while longer, under my observation."

"But why? I feel great," she objected, playing with her hand.

"Yes, but you might take a turn for the worse."

"Then I shall come back."

"You must agree that I am better equipped to judge when you may leave here," Kern said sternly. "Do not forget, you would have been nothing without me."

"I have already thanked you. But I am not a little girl and not a slave, and can do as I please!"

"Oho, she has a temper!" Kern realized with surprise.

"We shall discuss this later," he said. "In the meantime, please go to your room. John has probably already served your broth."

Briquet pouted, rose and left, not looking at Kern.

Briquet usually dined with Lauran in her room. When Briquet entered, Lauran was already at the table. Briquet sat down and made a careless, elegant gesture with her right hand. Lauran had noticed this gesture several times and wondered whether it belonged to the body of Angelica Gaye or to Briquet? Could Angelica Gaye's body have retained any of the automatic movements, somehow secured in the nervous system?

These questions were too complicated for Lauran.

86

"The physiologists are certain to be interested in this," she thought.

"Broth again! I am so tired of this hospital fare," Briquet said capriciously. "I would love a dozen oysters with a glass of Chablis." She sipped some broth from the cup and continued, "Professor Kern had just told me that he won't let me out of the house for a few more days. I don't think so! I am not a domestic bird. I can die of boredom around here. No, my kind of life is when there are lights, music, flowers, champagne, and everything spins like a whirlwind."

Chattering away, Briquet quickly finished her dinner, rose from her chair and walked over to the window.

"Good night, Mademoiselle Lauran," she said, glancing back. "I shall go to bed early today. Please do not wake me tomorrow. In this house, sleep is the best way to spend the time."

She nodded and went to her room.

Lauran sat down to write a letter to her mother.

All of her letters were checked by Kern. Lauran knew how strictly he was watching her and never even tried to send a letter by-passing his censure.

In order to avoid worrying her mother, she decided not to write her the truth about her involuntary confinement, even if she didn't have her letters read by Kern.

That night Lauran slept very poorly. She tossed and turned for a long time, thinking about the future. Her life was in danger. What would Kern do to "disarm" her?

Briquet must have been awake too. There was rustling in her room.

"She is trying on her new dresses," Lauran thought. Then all became quiet. Vaguely, when half-asleep, Lauran heard a subdued cry and woke up. "My nerves are completely out of control," she thought and fell back asleep.

She woke up at seven in the morning, as usual. Briquet's room was quiet. Lauran decided not to bother her and went to see Tomas. Tomas' head was as grim as ever. After Kern "sewed" Briquet's head onto a body, Tomas became even more depressed. He asked, begged, demanded to also be given a new body, to the point of becoming very rude. Lauran did all she could to calm him down. Having finished the morning ministrations with Tomas' head, she sighed with relief and went to Dowell's room. He met her with a welcoming smile.

"Life is a strange thing!" Dowell's head said. "Only recently I wanted to die. But my brain continues to work, and as recently as three days ago I had a very bold and original idea. If I could realize it, it could revolutionize medicine. I told Kern about it and you should have seen how his eyes flashed. He must have imagined a monument erected for him by thankful contemporaries during his life. And so, I must live – for him, for the idea, and for myself as well. It's almost like a trap."

"What is your idea?"

"I shall tell you, when I have solidified it better in my mind."

At nine, Lauran decided to knock on Briquet's door but there was no answer. Worried, she tried to open the door, but it was locked on the inside. Lauran had no choice but to inform Professor Kern.

As usual, Kern acted quickly and decisively.

"Break down the door!" he ordered John.

The African shoved with his shoulder. The door cracked and popped off the hinges. Kern, Lauran and John entered the room.

Briquet's bed was empty. Kern ran up to the window. A rope made of a torn sheet and two towels descended from the window frame to the ground. The flowerbed under the window was damaged.

"It's your trick!" Kern shouted, turning menacingly toward Lauran.

"I assure you, I had nothing to do with Mademoiselle Briquet's escape," Lauran said firmly.

"We shall discuss this later," Kern replied, although Lauran's determined answer had already convinced him that Briquet acted without any co-conspirators. "Our present problem is to find the escapee."

Kern went to his study and paced around the room anxiously. His first thought was to call the police. But he immediately abandoned it. Police must not be involved. He would have to appeal to private detective agencies.

"Damn it, it's my fault. I should have taken measures to guard her! But who could have thought! Yesterday's corpse has run away!" Kern laughed in frustration. "And now she'll spill everything that's happened to her. She did want to create a furor. This story will make it into the hands of reporters and then... I shouldn't have shown her to Dowell's head. What a handful. Some thanks I get!"

Kern called a private detective, handed him a large sum to cover expenses, offered even more in case of success and gave him a detailed description of the missing woman.

The detective examined the window and the tracks leading to the iron fence around the garden. The fence was tall and ended with sharp metal spikes. The detective shook his head, "Damn girl is a trooper!" On one of the spikes he noticed a piece of gray silk, which he picked up and carefully put away in his wallet.

"This was the dress she wore on the day of escape. We shall look for the woman in gray."

Having assured Kern that "the lady in gray" would be found in no more than twenty-four hours, the detective left.

He was an experienced man, one of the best in his profession. He found out Briquet's last address and the addresses of several of her friends, met them all, found Briquet's photo at one of their apartments and also found out where she used to perform. Several other agents were sent to all these clubs to look for the escapee.

"This bird couldn't have flown too far," the detective said confidently.

However, he was mistaken. Two days passed, and he still had no trace of Briquet. Only on the third day of the search, a man who frequented one small bar on Montmartre told the detective that the "resurrected" Briquet was there on the night of her escape. But then she vanished and no one knew where to.

Kern was growing more and more anxious. He was not only afraid that Briquet might tell others about his secrets, but of losing a valuable "exhibit". Of course, he could make another one out of Tomas' head, but that required time and tremendous energy. And the new experiment may not have concluded as gloriously. Demonstrating the revived dog would not have the same effect. No, Briquet had to be found no matter what. And he doubled and tripled the reward for finding the "escaped exhibit".

Every day, new agents reported to him about the results of their search, but the results were undesirable at best. It was as if Briquet fell off the edge of the Earth.

THE FINISHED SONG

When, with the help of her new strong and agile body, Briquet climbed over the fence and made her way to the street, she hailed a taxi and gave a strange address.

"Pere Lachez Cemetery."

But before she reached the Bastille square, she switched cabs and went to Montmartre. She "borrowed" Lauran's purse with a few dozen franks for her initial expenses. "Plus, one more sin is no big deal, and besides, it is necessary," she reasoned with herself. Confessing her sins has been postponed for a long time. She once again felt herself a whole, living, healthy person, and younger than before. Prior to the surgery, according to her own feminine count she was approaching thirty. But her new body was barely over twenty years old. The glands of the body rejuvenated Briquet's head, wrinkles vanished from her face and her complexion improved. "Life is good," Briquet thought, gazing dreamily into the small mirror she found in the purse.

"Stop here," she told the driver and, having paid him, walked the rest of the way.

It was almost four in the morning. She came to the familiar nightclub *Chat Noir* where she was performing that fateful night, when the stray bullet interrupted the merry tune she was singing. The club's windows were still brightly lit.

Not without trepidation Briquet entered the familiar vestibule. The tired doorman did not recognize her. She quickly went into a side door and followed a corridor to the dressing rooms adjacent to the stage. The first person she ran into was Red Martha. Martha screamed in fright and hid in her dressing room. Briquet laughed and knocked on the door, but Red Martha refused to open.

"Hey, Martlet!" Briquet heard a male voice. She was known by that nickname at the night club for her fondness of the brand of cognac with a martlet on its label. "You are alive. We have long since given you up for dead!"

Briquet turned and saw a handsome elegant man with a very pale clean-shaven face. Such pale skin is typical for people who rarely see the sun. It was Jean, Red Martha's husband. He didn't like to talk about his profession. His friends and drinking buddies considered it poor manners to ask about his sources of income. It was enough that Jean frequently had money and that he was a "great guy". On the evenings when Jean's pockets were stuffed with cash, wine flowed like a river and Jean paid for everything.

"Where did you come from, Martlet?"

"From a hospital," Briquet replied.

Afraid that friends or relatives of the woman whose body she now had might take it away, Briquet decided not to tell anyone about the unusual surgery.

"I was in a very serious condition," she continued making up her story. "I was given up for dead and even sent to the morgue. But then a medical student was examining my body, took my hand and felt a weak pulse. I was still alive. The bullet went next to my

93

heart but didn't damage it. I was instantly sent to a hospital and everything ended well."

"Splendid," Jean exclaimed. "Everyone will be terribly surprised. We must celebrate your resurrection."

The door lock clicked. Red Martha, who was eavesdropping on the conversation from behind the door, became convinced that Briquet wasn't a ghost and opened the door. The two friends hugged and kissed.

"You seem to be thinner, taller and more graceful, Martlet," Red Martha said, looking over the figure of her friend with curiosity and some surprise.

Briquet felt somewhat awkward under this searching gaze.

"Of course I am thinner," she said. "I was fed nothing but broth. As for my height, I bought shoes with very high heels. And the dress…"

"But why did you come here so late?"

"Oh, it's a whole other story… Have you performed already? Can you sit with me for a few minutes?"

Martha nodded. The two friends sat down at the dressing table with a big mirror and covered with boxes with eye pencils, makeup, perfume bottles, powder boxes, various little boxes with pins and needles.

Jean settled nearby, smoking an Egyptian cigarette.

"I ran away from the hospital. Like a proper fugitive," Briquet said.

"But why?"

"I got sick of broth. Broth, broth, broth, and more broth... I was practically drowning in broth. And the doctor wouldn't let me go, because he wanted to show me to medical students. I am afraid police shall be looking for me. I can't go to my place and was wondering whether I could stay with you. Of course, the best thing would be to leave Paris entirely for a few days. But I don't have enough money."

Red Martha clasped her hands – it was all so exciting.

"Of course you shall stay with me," she said.

"I think police might be looking for me too," Jean said thoughtfully, puffing out a ring of smoke. "I should vanish for a few days."

Martlet was a close friend, and Jean did not hide his profession from her. Martlet knew that Jean was an "important bird". His specialty was breaking into safes.

"Let's fly to the south with us, Martlet, You, Martha and I. To the Riviera to have some sea air. I've been indoors far too long, and I need some fresh air. If you can believe it, it's been two months since I've seen the sun and I am beginning to forget what it looks like."

"Wonderful," Red Martha clapped her hands.

Jean glanced at his expensive gold watch, "We still have an hour. Damn it, you must finish your song for us. And then we'll fly and they can look for you all they want."

Briquet accepted the idea with pleasure.

Her performance caused as much of a furor as she expected.

Jean stepped out onto the stage and recalled the tragic episode that took place several months prior, and then announced that Mademoiselle Briquet came back to life by popular demand after he, Jean, poured a shot of cognac *Martlet* down her throat.

"Martlet! Martlet!" the audience roared.

Jean waved to hush the audience and when the noise subsided, he continued, "Martlet shall sing her little song from the very same place where she was so suddenly interrupted. Band, *Kitty-Cat!*"

The band played from the middle of the verse, and Briquet finished her song to a round of applause. It was so noisy that she couldn't hear her own voice, but she didn't care. She felt happier than ever and reveled in the fact that everyone remembered her and met her so warmly. The fact that the warmth was partly due to the wine vapors didn't bother her a bit.

When she finished her song, she made an unexpectedly graceful gesture with her right hand. This was new. The audience applauded even louder.

"Where did she get this from? Such elegant manners. I must learn this gesture," Red Martha thought.

Briquet stepped down from stage into the audience. All the women hugged and kissed her, everyone held out their glass to clink with hers. Briquet was flushed and here eyes were shining. Success and wine turned her head. Having forgotten about the danger of pursuit, she was ready to stay there all night. But Jean never lost control, even when he drank as much as everyone else.

He checked his watch from time to time and finally walked up to Briquet and touched her hand, "It is time!"

"But I don't want to go. You may go without me. I am staying," Briquet replied, rolling her eyes.

Then Jean silently picked her up and carried her to the exit. The audience murmured.

"The show is over!" Jean shouted from the doorway. "Until next Sunday!"

He carried the struggling Briquet to the street and handed her into a waiting car. Martha joined them shortly with a few small suitcases.

"To the Republic Square," Jean said to the driver, not wishing to indicate his final destination. He was used to traveling with many transfers.

A MYSTERIOUS WOMAN

The waves of he Mediterranean splashed rhythmically against the sandy beach. A light breeze billowed the sails of white yachts and fishing boats. In the blue depths above, gray hydroplanes rumbled gently as they made short tourist flights between Nice and Mentone.

A young man in a white tennis suit sat in a wicker armchair reading a paper. Next to the chair was a tennis racket in its case and several recent issues of English scientific magazines.

Next to him, under an enormous white umbrella, his friend Armand Laret, who was an artist, was setting up an easel.

Arthur Dowell, the son of the late Professor Dowell, and Armand Laret were best friends, and this friendship was the best proof of the proverb that opposites attract.

Arthur Dowell was quiet and somewhat cool. He liked order and was capable of studying diligently and systematically. He was still a year away from graduation, but he was already offered a position at the Biology Department at his university.

Laret, like a true southern Frenchman, had an extremely impulsive character, disorganized and chaotic. He abandoned his paints and brushes for weeks, only to renew his work obsessively, when no power could pull him away from the easel.

The two friends were alike in one way: they were both talented and capable of reaching their goals, even though they approached these goals in different ways – one by large leaps and the other by steady walking.

Arthur Dowell's papers in biology had already attracted the attention of some of the greatest specialists in the field, and he was promised a glorious scientific career. Laret's paintings were much discussed at the exhibits, and some of them had already been purchased by some of the largest museums in the world.

Arthur Dowell threw down the newspaper, leaned back in his armchair and said, "Angelica Gaye's body still hasn't been found."

Laret shook his head inconsolably and sighed heavily.

"You still cannot forget her?" Dowell asked.

Laret turned to face Arthur so quickly that the latter smiled despite himself. It wasn't a passionate artist that stood before him any longer, but a knight armed with a shield-palette and a spear-maulstick in his right hand – an offended knight prepared to slay anyone who dealt him a mortal insult.

"Forget Angelica!" Laret shouted, raising his "weapons", "Forget her, who..."

A wave snuck up on him with a hiss and doused his legs almost to the knee. He finished sadly, "How could anyone forget Angelica? The world has grown dull since her voice has been silenced."

Laret found out about the death, or rather about the disappearance of Angelica Gaye when he was in London, where he went to paint a series of pieces called *The London Fog Symphony*. Laret wasn't just a fan of her talent, but also her friend and her knight. He was born in Southern Provence, among the ruins of medieval castles, and it showed in his romantic sensibilities.

When he found out that Gaye was in a train crash, he was so shocked that he interrupted one of his painting binges for the first time in his life.

Arthur, who came to London from Cambridge, decided to try and distract his friend from his dark thoughts and came up with a trip to the Mediterranean.

But even there, Laret couldn't find peace. When they returned from the beach to the hotel, he changed and boarded a train to go to the most crowded place – a Monte Carlo casino. He wanted to forget himself.

Despite the comparatively early hour, there was already a crowd in front of the low sprawling building. Laret went into the first hall, which was half-empty.

"Make your game," the croupier invited, armed with the little spatula for pulling in the money.

Laret passed into the next hall, whose walls were painted with scenes portraying half-nude women engaged in hunting, racing and fencing – all things associated with gambling and excitement. The paintings were infused with the spirit of struggle, passion, and greed; but all these feelings were even more prominent on the faces of the living people gathered around the table.

There was a fat businessman with a pale face, holding out money with his shaking freckled hands covered with reddish hair.

He was breathing heavily, as if he had asthma. His eyes were following the spinning ball. Laret could see the unmistakable signs that the man had lost a great deal and was now betting his last money hoping to win it back. And if not, perhaps this man would go to the suicide alley and pay his one last bill.

Behind the fat man stood a badly-dressed old man with tangled gray hair and maniacal eyes. In his hands were a notebook and a pencil. He kept writing down the winning and losing numbers and making calculations. He had long since lost his fortune and became a slave to the roulette. The casino administration paid him a small monthly pension to live on and gamble – a kind of advertisement. Presently, he was creating his own theory of probability, studying the fanciful nature of the fates. Whenever he made a mistake in his theories, he angrily struck his notebook with the pencil, mumbled something, and even hopped on my foot before going back to his calculations. But when his suppositions were proven correct, his face shone, and he turned to look at the people next to him as if wishing to say: see, I have finally established the laws of chance.

Two valets led in an old lady in a black silk dress, with a diamond necklace around her wrinkled neck, and helped her settle into an armchair at the table. Her face was so thickly powdered that it could not grow pale. At the sight of the mysterious little ball deciding one's joy and misfortune, her deeply sunken eyes flashed with greed and her thin bejeweled fingers started shaking.

A young, beautiful, slender woman dressed in an elegant dark-green suit passed by the table and tossed a thousand-frank bill onto it carelessly, lost, chuckled carelessly and continued to the next hall.

Laret bet a hundred franks on red and won.

"I must win today," he thought and bet a thousand – and lost. Nevertheless, he was convinced that he would win in the end. He had already succumbed to the gambling spirit.

Three people came up to the roulette table: a tall and imposing man with a very pale face and two women – a redhead and another one, in a gray suit. Laret glanced at her briefly and felt an indistinct anxiety. Before he realized what bothered him, the artist started watching the woman in gray and was struck by the movement she made with her right hand. "This looks familiar! Yes, Angelica Gaye had a movement like that!" The thought was so shocking that he could no longer gamble. Almost forgetting to collect his winnings, Laret rose and followed the group.

At four in the morning someone knocked loudly on Arthur Dowell's door. Dowell begrudgingly threw on a robe and opened it.

Laret entered the room, dead on his feet. He dropped into an armchair exhaustedly and said, "I think I am going mad."

"What's the matter, old man?" Dowell exclaimed.

"The thing is… I don't even know how to tell you this. I've been gambling since yesterday until two in the morning. Losses followed wins. And suddenly I saw a woman and was so struck by a gesture of hers that I gave up gambling and followed her to the restaurant. I sat down at a table and asked for a cup of strong black coffee. Coffee always helps me when my nerves are out of control. The stranger was at the table next to mine. She was with a young man, well-dressed but not the kind I would trust with my wallet, and a rather vulgar red-haired woman. My neighbors were drinking wine and chatting away merrily. The stranger in gray started humming a tune. She turned out to have a squealing voice that was rather unpleasant. But suddenly she took several lower notes ..." Laret squeezed his head. "Dowell! It was the voice of Angelica Gaye. I would have recognized it out of a thousand."

"Poor man! This is what it's come to," Dowell thought. He gently put his hand onto Laret's shoulder and said, "You must have imagined it, Laret. You must calm down. It was an accidental resemblance."

"No, no! I assure you," Laret objected heatedly. "I started looking at her carefully. She was fairly pretty, with a clear profile and sweet mischievous eyes. But her figure, her body! Dowell, may demons tear me to pieces with their teeth, if her figure wasn't identical to that of Angelica Gaye."

"Listen, Laret, take a bromide pill, have a cold shower and go to bed. Tomorrow, or rather today, after you wake up."

Laret looked at Dowell reproachfully, "You think I am mad, don't you? Don't jump to conclusions. Listen to me. This is not everything. When the singer finished her little song, she gestured with her right hand like this. That was Angelica's favorite gesture – it was completely unique, unlike any other."

"What are you trying to say? Do you think that the unknown singer has Angelica's body?"

Laret rubbed his forehead, "I don't know… this really is driving me mad. But listen. The woman had a complex necklace around her neck, not even a necklace but an entire detachable collar decorated with small pearls, at least an inch and a half wide. Her dress was very low-cut. It revealed the mole on her shoulder – Angelica Gaye's mole. The necklace looked like a bandage. Above it was the head of a woman I've never met before, but below it was the familiar body of Angelica Gaye, which I studied to the smallest detail, line and shape. Don't forget, Dowell, that I am an artist. I can memorize the unique lines and individual peculiarities of a human body. I have done so many sketches of Angelica, and painted so many portraits of her, that I cannot be mistaken."

"But this is impossible!" Dowell exclaimed. "Angelica is…"

"Dead? That's the thing, nobody knows that. She vanished without a trace, or her body did. And now…"

"And now you meet Angelica's resurrected corpse?"

"O-o-o-h!" Laret groaned. "That's exactly what I was thinking."

Dowell rose and paced around the room. He knew there would be no going back to bed for him.

"Let us think logically," he said. "You said that your unknown little singer seemed to have two voices: one of her own, which was more than mediocre, and another of Angelica Gaye."

104

"The lower register – her incomparable contralto," Laret replied, nodding.

"But this is physiologically impossible. You don't suppose that a person can produce high notes with the upper ends of her vocal cords and the lower ones – with the lower ends, do you? The sound frequency depends on the tension in the vocal cords along their entire length. They are like strings – a string that is pulled tighter produces a greater number of vibrations when plucked, resulting in a higher sound. And vise versa. Also, if such a surgery was performed, one's vocal cords would be shortened, resulting in a very thin voice. And no one could sing after that anyway – the scars would have interfered with the proper vibration of the vocal cords and the voice would be very hoarse at best. No, it is absolutely impossible. Besides, in order to 'revive' Angelica's body, someone would have had to have a bodiless head."

Dowell suddenly paused, because he remembered something that confirmed Laret's suggestion to a degree.

Arthur had a chance to watch some of his father's experiments. Professor Dowell used to add a feeding solution heated to 98.6 degrees Fahrenheit into the veins of a dead dog. The solution had adrenaline in it, which caused the blood vessels to expand and contract. When the solution made it to the heart, it restored its activity, and the heart started pumping blood through the body once again. Gradually, circulation was restored and the animal came back to life.

"The most important reason of an organism's death," Arthur's father said, "is the interruption in blood and oxygen supply to the organs."

"Then a person can be revived as well?" Arthur asked.

"Yes," his father replied happily. "I believe I can realize this 'miracle' someday. That is what my experiments are leading up to."

Therefore, the revival of a corpse was possible. But was it possible to revive a corpse in which the body belonged to one person and the head – to another? Was such a surgery possible? Arthur doubted that. It was true that he had seen his father perform uncommonly bold and successful surgeries with tissue and bone transplants. But those weren't as complicated, and his father was a brilliant surgeon.

"If my father was alive, I might have believed that there was some truth to Laret's suggestion about someone's head on Angelica Gaye's body. Only my father would have dared to conduct such a complex and unusual surgery. Perhaps his experiments were continued by his assistants?" Dowell thought. "But it's one thing to revive a head or even an entire body. It's a completely different thing to attach the head of one person to the body of another."

"What are you planning to do next?" Dowell asked.

"I want to find the woman in gray, meet her and uncover the mystery. Will you help me?"

"Naturally," Dowell replied.

Laret shook his hand firmly and they started discussing their plan of action.

A MERRY OUTING

Some time later Laret became very well acquainted with Briquet, her friend and Jean. At one point he offered them an outing on a yacht and the offer was accepted.

While Jean and Red Martha chatted with Dowell on deck, Laret offered Briquet to go below deck and look at the passenger quarters. There were two rooms, and while they were not very large, there was a piano in one of them.

"Oh, you've got an instrument here!" Briquet exclaimed.

She sat down at the piano and played a foxtrot. The yacht rolled slowly. Laret stood by the piano, watching Briquet carefully and thinking how to start his investigation.

"Sing something," he said.

Briquet didn't have to be asked twice. She sang, casting coquettish gazes at Laret. She liked him.

"You have a very... strange voice," Laret said, looking searchingly at her face. "It is as if there are two voices in your throat, belonging to two different women."

Briquet was taken aback but caught herself quickly and laughed somewhat forcefully. "Oh yes! It's been that way since I was a little girl. One singing teacher thought I had a contralto and the other one – a soprano. Each trained my voice his own way and this is the way it came out. Besides, I had a cold just recently."

"It's an awfully long explanation for one fact," Laret thought. "And why was she so confused? My suppositions are becoming justified. Something is going on here."

"When you sing in the lower register," he said sadly, "it is as if I hear the voice of a good friend of mine. She was a famous singer. The poor girl died in a train crash. Much to everyone's surprise, her body was never found. Your figure reminds me of her, you could have been twins. If I didn't know better, I would have thought it was her body."

Briquet looked at Laret again, no longer trying to hide her fear. She realized that Laret was carrying on this conversation for a reason.

"There are many people who look a lot like each other," she said in a shaky voice.

"Yes, but I've never seen that level of similarity. And besides, your movements... That gesture with your right hand... And the way you raised your hands just now, as if to fix a thick mane of hair. Angelica Gaye had hair like that. And that was the way she would fix an unruly lock of hair at her temple. But you don't have long hair. Yours is cut short in accordance with the latest fashion."

"I used to have long hair once," Briquet said, rising. Her face was pale and the tips of her fingers were shaking noticeably. "It's stuffy here... Can we go back up?"

"Wait," Laret stopped her, every bit as anxious as she was. "I must speak to you."

He forced her into an armchair by a porthole.

"I am sick... I am not used to the pitching!" Briquet exclaimed, trying to leave. While pushing her back down Laret touched her neck, seemingly by accident, and pulled away the edge of her necklace. He saw a series of pink scars.

Briquet fell back. Laret barely managed to catch her; she was in a swoon.

Not knowing what to do, the artist sprinkled water into her face from a carafe on a table nearby. She soon recovered. Indescribable terror flashed in her eyes. They gazed at each other for a few long moments. Briquet thought that the hour of retribution has come – the terrible hour when she would have to pay for taking someone else's body. Briquet's lips shifted and she barely whispered, "Don't kill me! Have pity."

"Calm down, I have no intention of killing you. But I must know your secret." Laret took Briquet's limp hand and squeezed it hard. "Admit it, this is not your body? Where did you get it from? Tell me the truth!"

"Jean!" Briquet tried screaming, but Laret covered her mouth with his hand and hissed into her ear, "If you scream one more time, you will not leave this room."

He then left Briquet in the armchair, locked the door of the cabin and firmly shut the porthole.

Briquet burst into tears like a child, but Laret was nonplussed.

"Tears won't help you! Tell me now, before I lose patience."

"It is not my fault," Briquet said, sobbing. "I was killed. And then I was revived. Just my head on a glass table... It was terrible!

And Tomas' head was there too. I don't know how it was done. It was Professor Kern who revived me. I asked him to give me another body, and he promised... And brought this body from somewhere..." she looked at her own shoulders and arms in terror. "But when I saw the dead body, I refused... I was so scared... I didn't want to, I begged him not to attach my head to the body. Lauran can confirm this – she took care of us. But Kern didn't listen. He put me to sleep, and I only woke up after the surgery. I didn't want to stay with Kern and ran away to Paris, and then here. I knew that Kern would follow me. I beg you, don't kill me and don't tell anyone. I don't want to be without a body again, it became my own. I have never felt such ease of movement. My leg hurts, but it will get better... I don't want to go back to Kern!"

As he listened to this disjointed narrative, Laret thought, "It sounds like Briquet is really not to blame. But Kern... How did he get the body of Angelica Gaye and use it for such a terrible experiment? Kern! I have heard that name from Arthur. Kern was his father's assistant, I think. We have to get to the bottom of it."

"Stop crying and listen to me carefully," Laret said sternly. "I shall help you, but on one condition – you mustn't tell anyone about what happened to you up until this moment. No one, except one person who will be here shortly. It's Arthur Dowell. You have already met him. You must do exactly as I tell you. If you don't, you will be in terrible trouble. You are an accomplice in a crime punishable by death. And there is nowhere you can go to hide your head and the body you have taken. You shall be found, tried

111

and guillotined. Listen to me. First of all, calm down. Second, go back to the piano and sing. Sing as loudly as you can, so that your friends could hear you. You are in a great mood and have no intention of returning above deck."

Briquet came up to the piano, sat down and started singing, accompanying herself with barely moving fingers.

"Louder and happier," Laret commanded, opening the porthole and the door. It was a very strange song – a kind of scream of terror and despair in a minor key.

"Slam the keys louder! Good! Keep playing and wait. You are coming to Paris with us. Don't you dare run. In Paris you shall be out of danger, we'll manage to hide you."

Laret came above deck looking as happy as ever.

The yacht was gliding smoothly through the waves, listing slightly to the right. The moist sea breeze helped Laret clear his head. He came up to Arthur Dowell, quietly pulled him to the side and said, "Go to the cabin and ask Mademoiselle Briquet to tell you what she told me. And I shall entertain our guests."

"How do you like the yacht, Madam?" he addressed Red Martha to distract her with a casual chat.

Jean was sprawled in a wicker chaise lounge and enjoyed his time away from police and detectives. He had no desire to think or observe. All he wanted to do was forget about his usual caution for a time. As he sipped excellent cognac from a small shot glass, he gradually went into a contemplative, half-dreamy state, which was perfect for Laret's purposes.

Red Martha was feeling great. Hearing her friend's singing from the cabin, she joined in between sentences and repeated the playful tune.

Whether Briquet had soothed herself by playing and singing, or Arthur appeared less dangerous to her, but she told him the story of her death and resurrection much more sensibly and coherently.

"And that was that. Is it really my fault?" she asked with a smile and sang a short little song *Is it my fault*, repeated by Martha on deck.

"Describe to me the other head that lived at Professor Kern's," Dowell said.

"Tomas?"

"No, the one Professor Kern took you to see after the surgery. Although…"

Arthur Dowell quickly pulled out his wallet, dug through it, pulled out a photograph and showed it to Briquet.

"Tell me, does this man look like the head of my… acquaintance you saw at Kern's?"

"Yes, that's him, exactly!" Briquet exclaimed. She stopped playing. "Amazing! He has shoulders. He has a body. Did he get a body too? What is the matter, my dear?" she asked sympathetically, startled by his reaction.

Arthur staggered back. His face blanched. He barely managed to make a few steps, dropped into an armchair and covered his face.

113

"What is the wrong?" Briquet asked him once again.

He said nothing. Then his lips moved, "Poor father," but Briquet couldn't hear him.

Arthur Dowell recovered very quickly. When he looked up, his face was almost calm.

"Forgive me, I must have frightened you," he said. "I sometimes have small heart episodes. It's all right now."

"But who is this man? He looks like... Is he your brother?" Briquet asked.

"Whoever he is, you need to help us find that head. You shall come with us. We'll set you up somewhere quiet, where no one will find you. When can you leave?"

"Today if needed," Briquet replied. "You won't... take my body from me, will you?"

Dowell didn't understand right away, then smiled and said, "Of course not, but only if you follow instructions and help us. Let's go back on deck."

"How is your trip?" he asked merrily, once above deck. He then glanced at the horizon with the air of an experienced sailor, shook his head anxiously and said, "I don't like this. See that dark strip at the horizon? If we don't get back in time, then..."

"Oh, then let us turn back now! I don't want to drown," Briquet exclaimed only half joking.

There was no storm in the forecast. But Dowell decided to frighten his land-faring guests to get back to shore.

114

Laret arranged to meet Briquet at the tennis court after dinner, "as long as there is no storm." They separated for a few hours.

"Listen, Laret, we have stumbled upon some great secrets," Dowell said, when they returned to the hotel. "Do you know whose head Kern is keeping at his house? The head of my father, Professor Dowell!"

Laret, who was settled on a chair, bounced back up like a ball.

"A head? A living head of your father? But how is that possible? That Kern! I'll rip him to shreds! We shall find your father's head."

"I am afraid we won't find it alive," Arthur replied sadly. "My father has proven the possibility of reviving heads separated from their bodies, but these heads only lived an hour and a half, and then died because the blood coagulated and the artificial feeding solutions couldn't keep them alive."

Arthur Dowell didn't know that shortly before his death his father invented a substance called *Dowell 217*, and re-named by Kern to *Kern 217*. Added to the blood, the substance prevented coagulation and made prolonged existence of the head possible.

"Dead or alive, we must find my father's head. We must be off to Paris!"

Laret ran to his room to pack.

IN PARIS

After a quick dinner, Laret rushed to the tennis court.

Briquet was a bit late but very glad to see him waiting. Despite the fright he gave her, Briquet continued finding him a very handsome man.

"Where is your racket?" she asked in disappointment. "Aren't you going to teach me today?"

For several days Laret has been teaching Briquet to play tennis. She turned out to be a very capable student. But Laret knew the secret of this ability better than Briquet herself: she had the trained body of Angelica, who was a splendid tennis player. Once upon a time she taught Laret a few strikes. All he had to do now was bring the already-trained body in coordination with Briquet's untrained brain and solidify the body's movements. Sometimes Briquet's movements were hesitant and awkward. But quite often she was uncommonly deft. For example, she surprised Laret exceedingly, when she started "slicing" – he never taught her that. The adroit and difficult hit had been Angelica's pride of sorts. It was during tennis when Laret started feeling a kind of tenderness toward the "revived Angelica", as he sometimes called Briquet, although it was far from the adoration he felt toward Angelica.

Briquet stood next to Laret, shielding herself from the sun with the tennis racket – one of Angelica's poses.

"We won't play today."

"Pity! I wouldn't mind a round or two, even though my leg hurts more than usual," Briquet said.

"Come with me. We are going to Paris."

"Now?"

"Right away."

"But I must change and pack a few things."

"Very well. You have forty minutes and not a moment longer. We shall pick you up in a car. Go pack, quickly."

"She really is limping a bit," Laret thought as he watched Briquet walk away.

During their trip to Paris, Briquet's leg began hurting seriously. Briquet lay in her berth and moaned quietly. Laret comforted her as well as he could. The trip brought them even closer together. He did his best to convince himself that, in taking care of Briquet he was really looking after Angelica Gaye. But Briquet treated Laret's attention as entirely her own. She was very touched by it.

"You are so kind," she said sentimentally. "You really frightened me there, on the yacht. But I am no longer afraid of you." And she smiled so charmingly that Laret couldn't help but smile in return. That smile belonged entirely to the head – after all, it was Briquet's face that was smiling. She was making great progress without even noticing.

A small incident took place not far from Paris and pleased Briquet exceedingly, while greatly surprising the culprit. During a particularly strong surge of pain, Briquet held out her hand and said, "If only you knew how I suffer…"

Laret took the hand and kissed it. Briquet blushed and Laret became embarrassed.

"Damn it," he thought, "I think I kissed her. But it was Angelica's hand. But it was the head that felt the pain, then by kissing the hand I was expressing pity for the head. But the head feels pain because Angelica's leg hurts, whereas Angelica's pain is felt by Briquet's head..." He became completely confused and felt even more awkward.

"How did you explain your sudden departure to your friend?" Laret asked to change the subject.

"I didn't. She is used to my antics. She and her husband are returning to Paris soon. I would very much like to see her. Please bring her to visit." Briquet provided Red Martha's address.

Laret and Arthur Dowell decided to settle Briquet in a small empty house at the end of Avenue du Maine that belonged to Laret's father.

"Next to a cemetery!" Briquet exclaimed superstitiously, when the car drove by the Montparnasse Cemetery.

"That means you'll live a long time," Laret assured her.

"Is that a sign?" Briquet asked.

"It most certainly is."

She calmed down.

The patient was settled in a rather cozy room on a huge old-fashioned bed with a canopy.

Briquet sighed in relief, leaning back on a pile of pillows.

"You must have a doctor and a nurse," Laret said. But Briquet objected vehemently. She was afraid that strangers would report her.

With great difficulty Laret convinced her to show the leg to his friend, a young doctor, and to hire the butler's daughter to be the nurse.

"This butler has been serving us for twenty years. He and his daughter are completely reliable."

The doctor examined the red and swollen leg, prescribed compresses, soothed Briquet and stepped into another room with Laret.

"Well?" Laret asked, not without anxiety.

"There is nothing serious yet, but we have to watch it. I shall visit her every other day. She must remain completely still."

Laret visited Briquet every morning. One time he entered the room quietly. The nurse had stepped out. Briquet was either dosing off or lying with her eyes closed. It was strange; her face seemed to be getting younger and younger. Briquet looked no older than early twenties. Her facial features became softer and more delicate.

Laret walked up to the bed on tiptoe, leaned over, and gazed upon her face for some time… and then gently kissed her forehead. This time Laret did not analyze whether he was kissing Angelica's remains, Briquet's head, or all of Briquet.

Briquet opened her eyes slowly and looked at Laret, a faint smile flickered over her lips.

"How do you feel?" Laret asked. "Did I wake you?"

"No, I wasn't asleep. Thank you, I feel fine. If only it wasn't for the pain…"

"The doctor says there is nothing serious. Keep still and you'll be better soon."

The nurse entered. Laret nodded and left. Briquet followed him with a tender gaze. Something new entered her life. She wanted to get better, but not for the night clubs, dancing, singing, and the merry inebriated clients at *Chat Noir*. All that was gone, had lost its meaning and value. Dreams of a new kind of happiness filled her heart. Perhaps that was the greatest miracle of transformation that neither she nor Laret were aware of. The healthy virginal body of Angelica Gaye not only rejuvenated Briquet's head, but also changed the course of her thoughts. The flirtatious nightclub singer was turning into a modest girl.

KERN'S VICTIM

While Laret was entirely consumed by taking care of Briquet, Arthur Dowell gathered information about Kern's household. From time to time the two friends conferred with Briquet who told them everything she knew about the house and people who lived in it.

Arthur Dowell decided to act very carefully. Kern had to have felt suspicious of everything and everyone since Briquet's disappearance. It was unlikely that he would manage to catch him by surprise. It was necessary to conduct his investigation in such a way that Kern would not suspect until the last moment that he was under attack.

"We must act as cunningly as possible," he told Laret. "First of all we must find out where Mademoiselle Lauran lives. If she is not on Kern's side, she will help us much more than Briquet ever could."

It didn't take much to find Lauran's address. But when Dowell went to the apartment, he was in for a disappointment. Instead of Lauran, he found only her mother – a neatly dressed handsome old woman on the verge of tears, clearly in a state of grief and disinclined to trust anyone.

"May I see Mademoiselle Lauran?" he asked.

The old woman looked at him in confusion, "My daughter? Do you know her? Whom do I have the honor of talking to and why do you want to see my daughter?"

"May I come in?"

"Please." Madam Lauran led the visitor into the small sitting room furnished with old-fashioned comfortable furniture, with armchairs in white covers with lace doilies over the backs. There was a large portrait on the wall. "She is an attractive girl," Arthur thought.

"My name is Radier," he said. "I am a country doctor and have only just come from Toulon. I used to know one of Mademoiselle Lauran's university friends. I ran into her when already in Paris and found out from her that Mademoiselle Lauran was working with Professor Kern."

"What is the name of my daughter's university friend?"

"Her name? Riche!"

"Riche, Riche! I have never heard of her," Madam Lauran noted, clearly unconvinced, then asked, "Were you sent by Kern?"

"No, I am not from Kern," Dowell replied with a smile. "But I would very much like to meet him. The thing is, he works in the area that is of great interest to me. I found out that he stages his most interesting experiments at home. But he is a very secretive man and doesn't want to let anyone into his sanctum."

Madam Lauran decided this sounded like truth; ever since she started working for Professor Kern her daughter had told her that he led a secluded life and never saw anyone. "What does he do?" she asked her daughter and received a vague answer, "Various scientific experiments."

"And so," Dowell continued, "I decided to meet Mademoiselle Lauran first and ask for her advice as to how I might go about

122

meeting Professor Kern. She could help pave the way for me and talk to Professor Kern about introducing me."

The young man's looks inspired trust, but everything related to Kern inspired such anxiety and unrest in Madam Lauran's soul, that she didn't know how to continue the conversation. She sighed heavily and barely keeping from crying said, "My daughter is not at home. She is in a hospital."

"In a hospital? What hospital?"

Madam Lauran couldn't stand it any longer. She has been alone with her grief for far too long and so, forgetting all caution, she told her guest everything: her daughter's sudden letter that her work required for her to stay at Kern's house to take care of difficult patients; her own fruitless attempts to see her daughter at Kern's house; her worries; and finally, Kern's informing her that her daughter had a nervous breakdown and was taken to a clinic for mentally ill patients.

"I hate Kern," the old lady said, wiping her eyes. "He drove my daughter to madness. I do not know what she saw at Kern's house and what she did – she wouldn't tell even me about it – but I know that as soon as Marie took that job, she became very tense. I no longer recognized her. She came home pale and unsettled; she had lost her appetite and couldn't sleep. She had nightmares every night. She thrashed about and talked in her sleep about the head of some Professor Dowell and about Kern chasing her. Kern sends me my daughter's earnings by mail. It is a significant sum and he sends it regularly. But I do not touch that money. You can't buy health with money. I have lost my daughter…" and the old woman burst into tears.

"No, there cannot be any of Kern's accomplices in this house," Arthur Dowell thought. He decided to no longer conceal the true reason for his visit.

"Madam," he said, "I can now tell you honestly, that I have just as many reasons to hate Kern. I wanted to meet your daughter so that I could sort a few things with Kern and… uncover his crimes."

Madam Lauran gasped.

"Oh, don't worry, your daughter has nothing to do in these crimes."

"My daughter would sooner die than commit a crime," Madam Lauran replied proudly.

"I wanted to ask for Mademoiselle Lauran's help, but I can see that she herself needs help. I have reasons to believe that your daughter is not mad, but was placed in a mental institution on Professor Kern's instructions."

"But why? What for?"

"Exactly for the reason that your daughter would sooner die than commit a crime as you said. Apparently, Kern considered her dangerous."

Arthur Dowell didn't know Madam Lauran well enough and was afraid of her congeniality, and so he didn't tell her everything.

"Kern was conducting unlawful surgeries. Would you be so kind as to tell me which hospital Kern sent your daughter to?"

Madam Lauran was so emotional that she barely managed to speak coherently. Her words interrupted by sobs, she replied, "Kern refused to tell me that for a long time. He wouldn't let me into his house. I had to write him letters. He replied very cagily, tried to reassure me and convince me that my daughter was getting better and would soon come back to me. When my patience wore thin, I wrote to him that I would report him to the police, if he didn't tell me immediately where my daughter was. And then he told me the address of the hospital. It is located not far from Paris, in Squaw. The clinic is the private property of Doctor Ravineau. Oh, I have been there! But they didn't even let me into the courtyard. It is a real prison, surrounded by a stone wall. 'These are the rules we have,' the guard told me. 'We don't let anyone in, not even the parents.' I asked for a doctor on duty, but he told me the same thing. 'Madam,' he told me, 'visits by the relatives often disturbs the patients and worsens their mental state. I can only tell you that your daughter is feeling better.' And he slammed the gates in my face."

"I shall try to see your daughter. Perhaps, I'll manage to get her out of there."

Arthur wrote down the address and said good bye.

"I shall do everything possible. Believe me, I am as interested in this as if Mademoiselle Lauran was my sister."

Dowell left, accompanied by a variety of advice and good wishes.

Arthur decided to go see Laret. As his friend spent all his time with Briquet, Dowell went to Avenue du Maine. Laret's car was parked by the house.

Dowell quickly ran up to the second floor and entered the sitting room.

"Arthur, this is terrible," Laret said to him. He was extremely upset, paced around the room and ruffled his black curly hair.

"What is the matter, Laret?"

"Oh!" his friend groaned. "She ran away."

"Who?"

"Mademoiselle Briquet, of course!"

"Ran away? But why? Do calm down and tell me what happened!"

It wasn't easy to make Laret talk sensibly. He continued dashing about, sighing, groaning and gasping. It was nearly ten minutes before Laret finally spoke, "Yesterday Mademoiselle Briquet had been complaining about worsening pain in her leg since morning. Her leg was very swollen and turned blue. I called the doctor. He examined the leg and said that the situation had taken an abrupt turn for the worse. …That there was an onset of gangrene. She needed surgery. The doctor didn't want to operate at the house and insisted that she must be transferred to the hospital. But Mademoiselle Briquet refused. She was afraid that someone at the hospital would notice the scars on her neck. She cried and said that she had to go back to Kern. Kern had warned her that she should have stayed with him until she was fully

126

recovered. She was now punished for not listening to him. And she trusted Kern as a surgeon. 'If he managed to bring me back from the dead and give me a new body, he can cure my leg. It's nothing for him.' All my reasoning did nothing to convince her. I didn't want her to go to Kern. And so I decided to trick her. I told her I would take her to Kern myself, intending to take her to the hospital. But I also wanted to make sure that the secret of Briquet's 'resurrection' didn't come out sooner than necessary – I remembered your needs too, Arthur. And I left for an hour, no more, to make arrangements with the doctors I knew. I wanted to trick Briquet, but she ended up tricking me and the nurse. When I came back, she was gone. This is all that was left – this note on her nightstand. Here, read it." And Laret gave Arthur a sheet of paper with a few words scribbled on it with a pencil, clearly in a hurry, "Laret, forgive me, but there is no other way. I am going back to Kern. Do not try to visit me. Kern shall make me well, as he has already done once. I shall see you soon – this thought shall be my comfort."

"There is no signature."

"Notice," Laret said, "the handwriting. It's Angelica's handwriting, although somewhat changed. Angelica would have written like this, if she was writing in poor light or if her hand was hurting: it is bolder and more sweeping."

"But what happened? How could she have escaped?"

"Alas, she ran away from Kern only to run away from me back to Kern. When I came back and discovered that the cage was

127

empty, I almost killed the nurse. But she explained that she was deceived herself. Briquet got up, went to the phone with great difficulty and supposedly called me. It was a trick. Of course she didn't call me. Having talked on the phone, Briquet told the nurse that I had arranged everything and was asking her to come to the hospital. Then she asked the nurse to get a taxi, got in with her help and left. She refused the nurse's help. 'It's not that far, and the hospital staff will take care of me once I get there,' she said. And the nurse was completely convinced that it was all done following my instructions and with my knowledge. Arthur!" Laret exclaimed suddenly, becoming agitated once again. "I am going to Kern immediately. I cannot leave her there. I have already called my car, it should be here by now. Come with me, Arthur!"

Arthur crossed the room. This was an unexpected complication! Suppose Briquet has already told them everything she knew about Kern's house. But her advice would be necessary in the future, not to mention that she was a living piece of evidence against Kern. Laret, in his present enraged condition, was going to be of no help.

"Listen, my friend," Arthur said, placing his hands onto the artist's shoulders. "Now more than ever, we must exercise control and abstain from any rash actions. It is done. Kern has Briquet. Should we bother the beast in his den too soon? Do you suppose Briquet will tell Kern about everything that has happened to her since she ran away from him? About our meeting with her and about how much we know about him?"

128

"I am convinced that she would not say anything," Laret replied confidently. "She promised me on the yacht and many times since then that she would keep the secret. She will now do so not only out of fear but for… other reasons."

Arthur knew these reasons. He had long since noticed Laret's attentions toward Briquet.

"Poor romantic," Dowell thought. "Tragic love affairs seem to be his credo. This time he is not only losing Angelica for the second time, but also his newly budding love. However, not all is lost yet."

"Be patient, Laret," he said. "Our goals are the same. Let us combine our efforts and play the game carefully. We have two options: either to deal Kern an immediate blow, or to try and find out about my father's head and about Briquet. Kern would have been on high alert after Briquet ran away from him. If he hadn't destroyed my father's head, he had probably concealed it very carefully. The head can be destroyed in minutes. As soon as the police start knocking on his door, he can eliminate all traces of his crime before they get in. And we won't find anything. Don't forget, Laret, Briquet is 'traces of crime' too. Kern performed unlawful surgeries. In addition, he stole Angelica's body, which is illegal. And Kern is a man who will stop at nothing. After all, he revived my father's head in secret from everyone. I know that my father allowed for his body to be used for scientific experiments in his will, but I never heard him agree to an experiment with his own head. Why is Kern hiding the existence of the head from everyone, even from me? What does he need it for? And why does he need Briquet? Perhaps he practices vivisection and Briquet is supposed to be his lab rat?"

"Then it's even more important that we rescue her quickly," Laret objected heatedly.

"Yes, rescue her but not accelerate her death. And our visit to Kern might bring about that undesirable outcome."

"Then what are we to do?"

"We must follow the second, more deliberate option. We shall do our best to make this path as short as possible. Marie Lauran can give us more useful information than Briquet. Lauran knows the layout of the house, she took care of the heads. Perhaps she had a chance to talk to my father… or rather, to his head."

"Then bring her over here."

"Alas, she too needs to be rescued."

"Does Kern have her?"

"He has her in a hospital. Apparently, in one of those hospitals where for a respectable sum of money one might lock up people who are as sick as you or I. We have a lot of work ahead of us, Laret." And Dowell told his friend about his meeting with Lauran's mother.

"Damn Kern! He spreads nothing but misery and horror around himself. If only I could lay my hands on him…"

"We'll do our best to make certain of that. Our first step is to talk to Marie Lauran."

"I'll go there immediately."

130

"That would be reckless. We must only become involved in person, when there is no other choice. In the meantime, we shall use the assistance of other people. You and I should form a kind of secret committee that governs the actions of reliable people, but remain unknown to the enemy. We must find someone we can trust who could go to Squaw, make friends with orderlies, nurses, cooks, and guards – anyone possible. If we manage to bribe even one of them, we'll be halfway there."

Laret was impatient. He wanted to get to action immediately, but he submitted to the more sensible Arthur and finally agreed to the more cautious strategy.

"But who can we ask? Oh, Shaub! He is a young artist, who has recently come from Australia. He is my friend, a great person and a fantastic athlete. He would treat this sort of mission as sport. Damn it," Laret cursed, "why can't I do it myself?"

"Why do you want to? Because it's so romantic?" Dowell asked with a smile.

RAVINEAU'S CLINIC

Shaub, a young, blond, pink-cheeked, athletic man of twenty-three, accepted the "conspirators'" proposal with delight. He wasn't given all the details yet, but was told that he could do a huge favor for his friends. He nodded, without even asking Laret, whether there was anything illegal about their undertaking – he believed in the honesty of Laret and his friend.

"Splendid!" Shaub exclaimed. "I am going to Squaw immediately. My sketch box will serve as a great excuse to justify a stranger coming to a small town. I shall ask the orderlies and the nurses to pose for me. If they are not too ugly, I'll try to hit on some of them a little."

"If you have to, offer your hand in marriage," Laret said enthusiastically.

"I am not handsome enough for that," the young man replied modestly. "But I shall be happy to use my biceps if necessary."

Their new ally set out on his way.

"Remember, act as quickly as you can but also be as careful as possible," was Dowell's last advice.

Shaub promised to return in three days. But he was back at Laret's house on the evening of the next day, extremely disappointed.

"Impossible," he said. "It's not a clinic, it's a prison with a wall. None of the staff go beyond the gates. All of the supplies are brought in by contractors who are not even allowed into the courtyard. Their building manager comes to the gate, takes stock of everything and has it all unloaded right there. I walked around that prison like a wolf around a sheepfold. But I didn't manage to get even a single peep over the stone fence."

Laret was disappointed and irked.

"I hoped," he said with poorly concealed irritation, "that you would be more inventive and enterprising, Shaub."

"Feel free to be inventive in my place," Shaub replied with equal frustration. "I would not have abandoned my attempts so quickly for no good reason. But I managed to meet a local artist, who knows the town well and has some clue about the clinic rules. He told me it was a very peculiar clinic. It concealed many crimes and mysteries behind its walls. Heirs place their wealthy relatives there for having lived much too long with no intention of dying, then declare them mentally ill and assume guardianship. Guardians of under-age heirs send their charges there just prior to their coming of age to continue 'managing' their fortunes freely. It is a prison for wealthy people, a life sentence for unfortunate wives, husbands, elderly parents and young heirs. The owner of the clinic, who is also the chief physician, receives colossal profit from the interested persons. His entire staff is well paid. Even law is helpless here, held back not by the stone wall but by gold. Everything rests on the foundation of bribery.

"You must agree, that I could sit in Squaw for a year and make not an inch of progress in getting into the clinic."

"You should have acted instead of sitting," Laret noted dryly.

Shaub raised one leg and pointed at the torn hem of his trousers.

"I did act, as you can see," he said with bitter irony. "Last night I tried to climb over the wall. It's not difficult. But before I had a chance to jump down on the other side, I was attacked by enormous Great Danes – and here is the result. Had I not been as agile as a monkey, they would have ripped me to shreds. At the same moment, the guards scattered all over the garden and there were electric lights everywhere. But that wasn't all. After I climbed back over the wall, the guards let their dogs loose. These animals are trained the same way they used to train dogs in southern American plantations to track down runaway slaves. Laret, you know how many races I have won. If I always ran as fast as I did last night to get away from the damn hounds, I would have been the world champion. Suffice it to say that I was able to hop onto the step of an automobile that was traveling at about twenty miles per hour, and that was the only thing that saved me!"

"Damn it! What are we going to do?" Laret exclaimed, ruffling his hair. "We shall have to call Arthur." He ran to the phone.

In just a few minutes, Arthur was shaking hands with his friends.

"We should have expected this," he said, having found out about Shaub's failure. "Kern knows how to bury his victims securely. What are we going to do?" he repeated Laret's question. "We could stage an all-out attack and use the same weapon as Kern – bribe the chief physician and…"

"I shall be happy to give up my entire fortune!" Laret exclaimed.

"I am afraid it might be insufficient. The thing is, the good doctor's commercial enterprise is driven by enormous amounts he received from his clients. That is on one hand. On the other hand he also has the trust of his clients, who are absolutely certain that if Ravineau received a good bribe, he would never sell them out. Ravineau doesn't want to undermine his reputation and thus compromise the entire foundation of his enterprise. Oh, he would do that, if he could receive a lump sum that equals all of his future income for the next twenty years. I am afraid that is not possible, even if we combine all of our fortunes. It is much simpler and cheaper to bribe some of his staff. But the problem is that Ravineau watches his staff just as carefully as he does his patients. Shaub is right. I made some inquiries about the clinic. It is easier for an outsider to get into a high-security prison and arrange an escape from there than to do the same with Ravineau's clinic. He hires people very selectively, primarily people who do not have any family. He also takes in those who are at odds with the law and want to hide from the watchful eyes of police. He pays well, but demands a commitment from all his employees to remain within the boundaries of the clinic for the duration of their service. The service term can be as long as ten or even twenty years."

"But where does he find people who agree to this almost life-long imprisonment?" Laret asked.

"He does. Many are seduced by the idea of setting themselves up for retirement. Many are brought there by poverty. Not everyone can stand it. Very rarely, once every few years, one or the other of Ravineau's employees escape. There was an incident just recently – an orderly couldn't stand the loss of his freedom and escaped. The same day his body was found in the vicinity of Squaw. Ravineau holds the local police in the palm of his hand. The official protocol stated that the orderly committed suicide. Ravineau took the corpse back to the clinic. We can only guess the rest. Ravineau probably showed the body to his other employees and made an appropriate speech, hinting that the same fate awaits anyone else who wants to violate the terms of the contract. And that was that."

Laret was astonished.

"Where did you get all this information from?"

Arthur smiled, very pleased with himself.

"You see," Shaub said, clearly relieved. "I told you it wasn't my fault."

"I can imagine the fun Mademoiselle Lauran is having in that accursed place. But what are we to do, Arthur? Blow up the walls with dynamite? Dig under?"

Arthur sat down in an armchair and thought. His friends waited. Suddenly Dowell exclaimed, "Eureka!"

"MADMEN"

A small room with a window looking out at the garden. Gray walls. Gray bed covered with a pale-gray fluffy blanket. A small white table and two chairs.

Lauran sat at the window and stared listlessly into the garden. Sunbeams turned her light-brown hair gold. She had grown much thinner and paler. From her window she could see an alley with groups of patients walking up and down. The nurses' white coats with black trim flickered between them.

"Madmen..." Lauran said quietly, looking at the patients. "I am mad too. How ridiculous! This is all I was able to achieve."

She painfully clenched her fists.

What happened?

Kern invited her to his study and said, "I must speak with you, Mademoiselle Lauran. Do you remember our first conversation, when you came here, looking for a job?"

She nodded.

"You promised to remain silent about everything you saw and heard in this house, did you not?"

"Yes."

"Repeat this promise and you may go see your mother. As you see, I trust your word."

Kern successfully picked the right string to pluck. Lauran felt very awkward. She was silent for several minutes. Lauran was accustomed to keeping her word, but after what she found out there… Kern saw her hesitation and anxiously waited for the outcome of her inner struggle.

"Yes, I promised you to remain silent," she finally said quietly. "But you deceived me. You concealed much from me. If only you told me the truth from the beginning, I wouldn't have promised you anything."

"Then you consider yourself free of your promise?"

"Yes."

"Thank you for your sincerity. It is easy to deal with you because at least you don't lie. You have the courage to speak the truth."

Kern did not say that just to flatter Lauran. Despite the fact that Kern considered honesty a form of stupidity, at that moment he really did respect her for the courage of her character and moral resilience. "Damn it, it is too bad that I have to get this child out of the way. But what else am I supposed to do with her?"

"So, Mademoiselle Lauran, you shall go and report me at the first opportunity. You know very well the consequences it will have for me I shall be executed. Besides, my name will be disgraced."

"You should have thought about it earlier," Lauran replied.

"Listen, Mademoiselle," Kern continued, as if not hearing her. "Abandon your narrow moral viewpoint. Understand, if it wasn't for me, Professor Dowell would have long since rotted in the grave or burned at the crematorium. His work would have stopped. What his head does here now is, essentially, posthumous work. And I made it happen. You must agree, that in this case I have certain rights to the head's 'production'. Besides, Dowell – his head – couldn't have realized his discoveries without me. You know that brain does not respond well to surgery and transplantation. Nevertheless the surgery of merging Briquet's head with a body worked beautifully. The area of the spinal cord passing through the neck vertebrae managed to heal. Dowell's head and Kern's hands worked together on solving this problem. And these hands," Kern held out his hands and looked at them, "are worth something. They saved many hundreds of human lives and shall save more, if only you put away your sword of retribution. But that is not all. Our latest work shall revolutionize not only medicine but all of human existence. From now on, medicine will be able to restore an extinguished human life. How many great people can be revived after their death, and have their lives prolonged to benefit all of humanity! I shall extend the life of a genius, give a father back to his children and a husband back to his wife. Eventually, every surgeon shall perform such operations. The sum of human suffering shall be diminished."

"At the cost of other unfortunates."

"Perhaps so, but where two are crying now, there will be only one. Where there are two corpses, there will be one. Is this not a great possibility? And does it not negate my personal matters, criminal as they may be? What patient cares whether a surgeon saving his life has a few questionable deeds upon his soul? You shall kill not only me, but thousands of other people I could save in the future. Have you thought of that? Your crime shall be a thousand times worse than mine, if indeed what I've done is a crime. Think it over and give me your answer. Now go. There is no rush."

"I have already given you my answer." And Lauran left the study.

She went to Professor Dowell's room and told him about her conversation with Kern. Dowell's head thought about it.

"Wouldn't it be better to conceal your intentions or at least give him an indefinite answer?" the head finally whispered.

"I cannot lie," Lauran replied.

"It gives you credit, but... you have doomed yourself. You might die, and your sacrifice shall be of no use to anyone."

"I don't know any other way," Lauran said, nodded to the head sadly and left.

"Dice are rolling," she kept repeating as she sat near the window of her room.

"Poor mom," she thought suddenly. "But she would have done the same thing," Lauran replied to herself. She wanted to write a letter to her mother and tell her everything that had happened to her. One last letter. But there was no way to send it. Lauran had no doubt that she was about to die. She was prepared to meet her end calmly. She was saddened only by the thoughts of her mother and by the fact that Kern's crime would remain secret. She believed, however, that sooner or later retribution would catch up to him.

What she expected took place a lot sooner than she thought.

Lauran turned off the light and went to bed. Her nerves were strained. She heard a rustling behind the armoire near the wall. The rustling surprised rather than scared her. The door to her room was locked. No one could enter in a way that she wouldn't hear it. "What is this noise? Mice?"

What happened next was dazzlingly fast.

The rustling was followed by a creaking. Someone's footsteps approached the bed. Lauran rose on her elbows, but at the same time, someone's strong hands pressed her down and covered her face with a chloroform mask.

"Death!" the thought flickered through her mind and, shivering all over, she instinctively tried to pull away.

"Calm down," she heard Kern's voice, very much like the one he used during regular surgeries, and then she fainted.

She came to at the clinic.

Professor Kern carried out the threat of "extremely unpleasant consequences", if she refused to keep his secret. She expected anything from him. But he took his revenge and remained unscathed. Marie Lauran sacrificed herself, but her sacrifice was pointless. That notion further violated her emotional balance.

She was approaching desperation. She felt Kern's influence even at the clinic.

During the first two weeks Lauran wasn't even allowed to go out into the large shady garden where "quiet" patients were allowed to walk.

141

The quiet ones were those who did not protest their imprisonment, did not try to prove to the doctors that they were completely healthy, did not threaten to go public, and made no attempts to escape. Only about ten percent of the clinic's patients were actually mentally ill, and most of them were driven mad at the clinic. For that purpose, Ravineau had a complex system of "psychiatric poisoning".

"A DIFFICULT CASE"

For Doctor Ravineau, Marie Lauran was a "difficult case". It was true that Lauran's nervous system was seriously impaired by working with Kern, but her will was not compromised. That was the challenge Ravineau decided to take upon himself.

He delayed Lauran's "treatment" at first, taking time to study her from a distance. Professor Kern did not give Doctor Ravineau any specific directions regarding Lauran: whether to drive her to premature death or drive her mad. The latter was more or less required by the system established by Ravineau at his clinic.

Lauran anxiously waited for her fate to be decided. Death or madness – there were no other options for her or the others. And she gathered all her mental powers to at least oppose the madness. She was very gentle, obliging and outwardly calm. But Doctor Ravineau could not be deceived by that façade, for he possessed extensive experience and a great talent as a psychiatrist. Lauran's obedience only made him more concerned and suspicious.

"Difficult case," he thought as he talked to Lauran during his usual morning rounds.

"How do you feel?" he asked.

"Very well, thank you," Lauran replied.

"We do everything possible for our patients, but the unusual environment and relative limitation of their freedom has a depressing effect on some patients. They experience a sense of loneliness and yearning."

"I am used to loneliness."

"It's not easy to win her confidence," Ravineau thought and continued, "You are essentially well. Your nerves are a bit out of order, that is all. Professor Kern told me that you had to participate in scientific experiments that could have a rather strong impression upon a fresh person. You are so young. You are overly tired and have a slight neurasthenia. Professor Kern, who values you very greatly, decided to give you a little vacation."

"I am very grateful to Professor Kern."

"A secretive character." Ravineau felt irritated. "I should get her to meet other patients. Perhaps she would become more open with them and let me study her quicker."

"You have been cooped up for too long," he said. "Why don't you go into the garden? We have a lovely garden, a park even – it is over twenty acres large."

"I am not allowed to go outside."

"Indeed?" Ravineau exclaimed in surprised. "It must be an oversight by one of my assistants. You are not one of those patients who would be harmed by going outside. Please, do go out. Meet other patients; there are some interesting people among them."

"Thank you, I shall take advantage of your permission."

When Ravineau left, Lauran walked out of her room and followed a long corridor painted in dull gray color with black trim

144

toward the exit. From behind locked door she could hear insane howling, shouts, hysterical laughter and mumbling.

"Oh...oh... oh..." came from the left.

"Oooooh... Ha-ha-ha-ha," was a response from the right.

"Like a zoo," Lauran thought, trying not to be influenced by this oppressive environment. She did quicken her steps somewhat and hurried out of the building. Before her was a smooth path leading into the garden and Lauran followed it.

Doctor Ravineau's "system" was felt even there. Everything bore a hint of darkness. The trees were predominantly evergreens, with dark needles. Wooden benches without backs were painted dark gray. Lauran was particularly struck by the flower beds. They were shaped like graves and the lowers were mostly pansies in shades of dark blue and almost funerary black, bordered by white daisies. Dark thujas completed the landscape.

"It's like a real cemetery. One would have thoughts of death despite himself. But you won't trick me, Monsieur Ravineau, I have guessed your secret and your 'effects' won't catch me by surprise," Lauran encouraged herself, quickly passing through the "funeral flower garden" and going into a pine alley. Tall trunks reached up like columns of a temple, topped by dark green domes high above. The tree tops rustled in an even, monotonous, dry noise.

Gray robes of the patients appeared here and there in various places around the park. "Which ones of them are crazy and which ones are normal?" Lauran wondered. That could be determined

145

fairly reliably by observing them. Those who were not yet hopeless were looking at the newcomer, Lauran, with interest. But the patients with entirely faded consciousness had shrunk within themselves and mentally cut themselves off from the outside world, at which they gazed with unseeing eyes.

A tall thin old man with a long gray beard approached Lauran. The man raised his bushy eyebrows, looked at Lauran and said as if continuing to talk to himself, "I counted for eleven years, and then lost count. There are no calendars here and time has stopped. I don't know for how long I've been walking up and down this alley. Perhaps twenty years, or maybe a thousand. In the eyes of God one day is like a thousand years. It is hard to tell time. And you too shall walk for a thousand years to the stone wall, and a thousand years back. There is no escape. Abandon all hope ye who enters here, as Monsieur Dante said. Ha-ha-ha! Are you surprised? Did you think I was mad? I am clever. Only madmen have the right to live here. But you are trapped here just as I am. You and I are..." seeing an approaching orderly, whose duties included eavesdropping on the patients' conversations, the old man winked and continued in the same tone, "I am Napoleon Bonaparte and my one hundred days have yet to come. Do you understand?" he asked, after the orderly was gone.

"Poor man," Lauran thought, "is he really pretending to be mad to avoid the death sentence? Apparently I am not the only one to put on a protective mask."

146

Another patient approached Lauran, a young man with a black goatee, and started mumbling some nonsense about taking a square root of squaring of the circle. That time the orderly did not bother coming closer to Lauran – apparently the young man did not inspire any suspicions with the administration of the clinic. He came up to Lauran and talked faster and more persistently, spitting as he went on, "A circle is infinite. Squaring of a circle is squaring of infinity. Listen carefully. To take a square root of squaring of a circle means to take a square root of infinity. That would be a fraction of infinity to the nth degree, therefore one could establish the squaring... But you are not listening to me," the young man became suddenly angry and grabbed Lauran's hand. She pulled away and almost ran to her dormitory. Not far from the door she ran into Doctor Ravineau. He was barely hiding a pleased smile.

The moment Lauran ran into her room, there was a knock on the door. She would have happily locked herself in, but there were no internal latches on the door. She decided not to answer. Nevertheless, the door opened and Doctor Ravineau appeared on the threshold.

His head was raised high, as usual, his large, round, somewhat bulging eyes peered carefully through the lenses of his pince-nez, his black mustache and goatee moved when he spoke.

"Forgive me for entering without invitation. My position as the Chief Physician gives me certain privileges."

147

Doctor Ravineau decided that the time was right to begin the "destruction of moral values". His arsenal included a variety of methods of influence – from disarming sincerity, courtesy and charming attentiveness to rudeness and cynical frankness. He decided to break Lauran's balance no matter what and assumed an unceremonious and mocking tone.

"Why do you not say, 'Please, come in, forgive me for not inviting you. I was deep in thought and did not hear you knock...' or something like that?"

"No, I heard you knock, but did not answer because I wanted to be alone."

"As truthful as usual!" he said ironically.

"Truthfulness is a poor object for irony," Lauran noted with some irritation.

"Jackpot," Ravineau thought happily. He sat down across from Lauran and leveled his unblinking lobster eyes at her. Lauran tried to withstand his gaze, but eventually she felt uncomfortable and lowered her eyes, blushing slightly from disappointment at herself.

"You suppose," Ravineau said in the same ironic tone, "that truthfulness is a poor object for irony. But I think that it is very suitable. If you were really honest, you would have kicked me out of here because you hate me; but in the meantime you attempt to keep a pleasant smile of a welcoming hostess."

"It is merely... politeness as the result of my upbringing," Lauran replied dryly.

"And had it not been for the upbringing, you would have kicked me out?" And Ravineau suddenly laughed in a high-pitched barking way. "Excellent! Very good! Politeness is out of sync with truthfulness. Therefore, you would compromise your truthfulness for the sake of politeness. One." And he bent one finger. "Today I asked you how you felt, and you said 'splendid', even though I could see in your eyes that you were fit to hang yourself. Therefore, you lied then as well. Was that out of politeness too?"

Lauran did not know what to say. She either had to lie or admit that she intended to conceal her feelings. And she said nothing.

"I shall help you, Mademoiselle Lauran," Ravineau continued. "It was a mask of self-preservation. Yes or no?"

"Yes," Lauran said defiantly.

"And so, you lie for the sake of good manners – one, and you lie for the sake of self-preservation – two. If we continue this conversation, I am afraid I might run out of fingers. You also lie out of pity. Did you not write soothing letters to your mother?"

Lauran was struck. Did Ravineau really know everything? It appeared that he did and that it too was included in his system. The clients who supplied him with fake patients were required to supply every bit of information about the reasons for their hospitalization, as well as everything about the patients themselves. The client knew that it was necessary and served their own interests, and it revealed every terrible secret to Ravineau.

"You lied to Professor Kern in the name of abused justice and wishing to punish the vice. You lied in the name of truth. What a bitter paradox! If we count it all up, we shall discover that your truth was being fed by lies each and every step of the way."

Ravineau hit the bull's eye. Lauran was crushed. It had never occurred to her that lies played such an enormous role in her life.

"In your spare time give some thought, my dear truth-lover, to the tally of your sins. And what did you reach with your truth? I shall tell you: you have reached this life sentence. There isn't a force on earth or in heaven that could get you out of here. As for the lies? We might consider the honorable Professor Kern a hound of hell and a father of lies, but he gets along quite splendidly."

Ravineau, who never took his eyes off Lauran, suddenly paused. "This should be enough for the first time, this was a good shot," he thought with satisfaction and left.

Lauran didn't even notice his absence. She sat covering her face with her hands.

Since that evening, Ravineau came to see her every day to continue his Jesuit conversations. To compromise Lauran's moral principles along with her psyche became for Ravineau a matter of professional pride.

Lauran suffered deeply and sincerely. On the fourth day she couldn't stand it, rose and screamed, "Get out of here! You are not a man, you are a demon!"

This scene brought great pleasure to Ravineau.

"You are making progress," he chuckled, remaining in his seat. "You are becoming much more truthful than before."

"Leave!" Lauran said, gasping.

"Splendid, she'll be fighting me soon," the doctor thought and left, whistling happily.

Lauran wasn't fighting yet and would have probably done so only if her mind became seriously jeopardized, but her mental health was nevertheless in great danger. When left alone, she realized in horror that she wouldn't last much longer.

Ravineau didn't miss a thing that could speed up the tragic outcome. In the evenings, Lauran started hearing the sounds of a sad song, performed on some unknown instrument. It was as if a cello wept somewhere, music sometimes rising into the higher register of a violin, and then changing not only the register but the timbre as well, and sounding like a human voice – clear, beautiful, but endlessly sad. The aching melody did a kind of a circle and then repeated itself.

When Lauran first heard the music she rather liked it. The music was so gentle and quiet that Lauran doubted whether someone was really playing somewhere, or whether she was developing auditory hallucinations. Minutes followed minutes, and the music continued around its enchanted circle. The cello was replaced by the violin, and the violin – by the longing human voice. A single note sounded forlornly in the accompaniment. In an hour, Lauran was convinced that the music did not exist and that it sounded only in her mind. There was no place to hide from the terrible melody. Lauran covered her ears, but she seemed to still hear the music – cello, violin, voice… cello, violin, voice…

"This could drive you mad," Lauran whispered. She tried singing and talking to herself to block the music, but nothing helped. The music pursued her even in her sleep.

"People can't play and sing endlessly. This must be mechanical music. Or I am delusional," she thought, lying in bed with her eyes wide open, unable to sleep and listening to the endless circle: cello, violin, voice… cello, violin, voice…

She couldn't wait until morning, when she could run off to the park, but the melody had already become an obsessive thought. And only the shouts, groans and laughter of the madmen walking in the park managed to obscure it somewhat.

A NEW PATIENT

Gradually Marie Lauran's nerves became so unstable that, for the first time in her life, she began contemplating suicide. During one of her walks she started thinking of a way to kill herself and became so absorbed in her thoughts that she did not notice a patient who came up to her and blocked her path, saying, "Blessed are those who know not of the unknown. It's all sentimentalism anyway."

Lauran was startled and looked up at the patient. He was dressed like everyone else, in a gray robe. Tall, dark haired, with a handsome fine-featured face, he immediately attracted her attention.

"He must be new," she thought. "Shaved no more than five days ago. But why does his face remind me of someone?"

Suddenly the young man whispered, "I know you, you are Mademoiselle Lauran. I saw your portrait at your mother's."

"How do you know me? Who are you?" Lauran said in surprise.

"There is very little to this world. I am my brother's brother. And my brother is me!" the young man shouted.

An orderly passed, giving him a discreet but careful glance. When he was gone, the young man whispered again, "I am Arthur Dowell, the son of Professor Dowell. I am not crazy, I am just pretending to get in..."

The orderly approached them once again.

153

Suddenly, Arthur ran away from Lauran, yelling, "Here is my belated brother! You are me and I am you. You became me after death. We were twins, but you died and I didn't."

And Dowell chased after some melancholiac who was scared by this sudden attack. The orderly ran after him, trying to protect the small sickly melancholiac from a violent madman. When they reached the end of the park, Dowell abandoned his victim and turned back to Lauran. He ran faster than the orderly. As he passed Lauran, Dowell slowed down and finished what he had to say.

"I am here to save you. Be prepared tonight," and dashing off to the side he started dancing around some crazy old lady who paid him not the slightest attention. He then sat down onto the bench, lowered his head and fell deep into thought.

He played his role so well, that Lauran was confused as to whether Dowell was only faking his madness. But hope has already trickled into her heart. She had no doubt that the young man was Professor Dowell's son. The similarity was so striking, even though the gray hospital robe and unshaved face significantly "obscured" Dowell. And he recognized her from the portrait. He must have seen her mother. All this sounded like truth. In any case, Lauran decided not to go to bed that night and wait for her unexpected savior.

The hope for escape inspired her and gave her new reserves of energy. It was as if she woke up from a terrible nightmare. Even the annoying song sounded quieter, moved away and seemed to dissolve in the air. Lauran sighed deeply, like a person who was let outside from a dark dungeon. Desire to live flared up in her with unprecedented force. She wanted to laugh. But now, more than ever, she had to be cautious.

When the breakfast gong rang, she did her best to keep her face despondent, which was her usual expression lately, and headed to the dormitory.

Doctor Ravineau stood by the entrance, as usual. He watched the patients like a jailor would watch his prisoners, as they returned to their cells. His eyes didn't miss a single thing: a stone hidden in a sleeve, a torn robe, a scratched hand or face. He watched their faces with particular care.

"How do you feel?" he asked.

"As usual," she replied.

"Adding another line to the list, I see. And in the name of what this time?" he asked ironically and added as she went in, "We'll have a chat in the evening."

"I expected depression. Is she becoming ecstatic? Apparently, I have missed something in the course of her thoughts and moods. I must find out what it is…" he thought.

In the evening he came over for that very purpose. Lauran was very afraid of this meeting. If she could stand it, it could be the last one. But if she couldn't, she would be lost. In her mind she called Doctor Ravineau "the Great Inquisitor". Had he lived a few centuries earlier, he would have worn the title with pride. She was afraid of his sophisms, his biased interrogation, his sudden trick questions, his astonishing knowledge of psychology, his devilish analysis. He truly was "the great logician", a modern Mephistopheles who could destroy all her moral values and shed enough doubt to demolish the most obvious truths.

To avoid betraying herself and thus signing her own death sentence, she decided to gather all her willpower and remain silent, no matter what he said. That too was a dangerous way. It was an open declaration of war, the last revolt in the name of self-preservation, which was bound to cause a stronger attack. But she had no other choice.

When Ravineau came, stared at her with his round eyes, as usual, and then asked, "Well then, why did you lie?" Lauran did not make a sound. Her lips were firmly pressed together and her eyes were lowered. Ravineau began his interrogation. Lauran alternatively turned pale or crimson, but remained silent. Ravineau started losing his patience and becoming angry, which happened to him very rarely.

"Silence is golden," he said mockingly. "Having lost all your other values, you wish to preserve at least this one virtue of animals and complete idiots, but you won't be able to. The silence shall be followed by an explosion. You will burst from anger if you don't open the safety valve of accusatory eloquence. And what is the point in being silent? Don't you think I can read your thoughts? 'You are trying to drive me mad,' you are thinking right now, 'but you will fail.' Let us be frank. I will not fail, my dear lady. To ruin a human soul for me is no harder than to damage a clock

156

mechanism. I know all the nuts and bolts of this uncomplicated machine by heart. The more you resist, the deeper and more hopeless shall be your downfall into the darkness of insanity."

"Two thousand four hundred sixty-one, two thousand four hundred sixty-two..." Lauran counted in her head to keep from listening what Ravineau was saying to her.

No one knows how long this torture would have continued, but a nurse knocked on the door.

"Come in," Ravineau said irately.

"The patient in room seven is dying," the nurse said.

Ravineau rose reluctantly.

"Just as well," he grumbled quietly. "We shall finish our interesting conversation tomorrow," he said, tipped Lauran's face up, snorted mockingly and left.

Lauran breathed a heavy sigh and slumped over the table, completely exhausted.

The music of hopeless longing was already playing behind the wall. The power of this entrancing music was so great that Lauran fell under its spell despite herself. She imagined that the meeting with Arthur Dowell was nothing but a product of her sick imagination and that any struggle was useless. Death, only death could spare her this torment. She looked around. But suicide was not something Doctor Ravineau included in his system. There wasn't even a hook to hang herself. Lauran shuddered. She suddenly remembered the face of her mother.

"No, no, I won't do it, for her sake I won't do it. Just this last night... I shall wait for Dowell. And if he doesn't come..." she did not finish the thought but felt with her entire being what would happen to her if he didn't fulfill the promise he gave her.

ESCAPE

This was the most tiresome night of all the ones Lauran had spent at Doctor Ravineau's clinic. Minutes went on as endlessly and tiresomely as the familiar music coming from behind the wall.

Lauran paced nervously from window to door. There were careful footsteps in the hallway. Her heart beat fast and then froze – she recognized the footsteps of the night-time nurse who came to each door to look through the spyhole. The two hundred lumen lamps burned in the corridor all night, because Doctor Ravineau decided it helped induce insomnia. Lauran quickly snuck into her bed, fully clothed, covered up with the blanket and pretended to sleep. And an odd thing happened: she, who couldn't sleep for many nights, suddenly fell asleep from the extreme fatigue of everything she went through lately. She slept only a few minutes, but she felt as if the entre night had passed. She jumped up in alarm, rushed to the door and suddenly ran into the entering Arthur Dowell. He kept his word. She barely kept from crying with joy.

"Quickly," he whispered. "The nurse is in the west corridor. Come."

He grabbed her hand and carefully led her behind him. Their footsteps were obscured by the groans and yells of the patients suffering from insomnia. The endless corridor finally ended at the door leading out of the building.

"There are guards in the park, but we should be able to sneak by them…" Dowell whispered quickly, pulling Lauran into the park.

"But the dogs…"

"I kept feeding them dinner leftovers and they know me. I have been here for some time, but stayed away from you to avoid suspicion."

The park was swathed in gloom. But at the stone wall there was a row of burning lights, like there would be in a prison.

"There are some shrubs over there. That's the way."

Suddenly Dowell fell down on the grass and pulled Lauran with him. She followed his example. One of the guards passed by the escapees. When he was gone, they continued on their way to the wall.

A dog growled somewhere, then ran up to them and wagged at the sight of Dowell. He tossed it a piece of bread.

"See," Arthur said, "the hardest part is done. Now we just have to climb over the wall. I shall help you."

"What about you?" Lauran asked anxiously.

"Don't worry, I'll follow you," Dowell replied.

"What happens after we get over the wall?"

"Our friends are waiting. Everything is ready. Please, a little bit of calisthenics."

Dowell leaned against the wall and boosted Lauran to the top.

At that moment, one of the guards saw her and raised alarm. Suddenly, the entire garden became lit. The guards ran toward them, calling each other and the dogs.

160

"Jump!" Dowell ordered.

"And you?" Lauran shouted.

"Jump, damn you!" he yelled and Lauran jumped. Someone's hands caught her.

Arthur Dowell jumped, grabbed the top of the wall and started pulling himself up. But two orderlies grabbed his legs. Dowell was so strong that he almost lifted them up with him. But one of his hands slipped and he fell down and knocked down the orderlies.

There was a noise of a car engine starting behind the wall. His friends must have been still waiting for him.

"Leave now! Go!" he shouted, wrestling with the orderlies.

The car horn beeped and he heard it pulling away.

"Let me go, I'll come with you," Dowell said, no longer resisting.

But the orderlies did not let go of him. They firmly grabbed his arms and took him to the dormitory. Doctor Ravineau stood by the door in his robe, puffing on a cigarette.

"To the solitary sell. Straightjacket!" he said to the orderlies.

Dowell was taken to a small room without windows and with walls padded with matrasses. It was used to contain violent patients during their fits. The orderlies threw Dowell on the floor. Ravineau followed them into the cell. He was no longer smoking. With his hands in the pockets of his robe he leaned over Dowell and stared at him with his round eyes. Dowell withstood his gaze. Then Ravineau nodded to the orderlies and they left.

"You are not a bad malingerer," Ravineau addressed Dowell, "but I am difficult to deceive. I had you figured out on the first day and had you watched, but, I admit, I could not guess your intentions. You and Lauran will pay dearly for this little prank."

"No more dearly than you," Dowell replied.

Ravineau's cockroach-like mustache moved, "A threat?"

"In response to a threat," Dowell said.

"I am a difficult enemy," Ravineau said. "I broke people stronger than a pup like you. Are you going to complain to the local government? It won't help, my friend. Besides, you might disappear before the representatives of law get here. There won't be a trace left. Besides, what is your real name? Du Barry was an alias, was it not?"

"Arthur Dowell, the son of Professor Dowell."

Ravineau was clearly surprised.

"I am very pleased to meet you," he said, trying to conceal his confusion behind ridicule. "I had the honor of knowing your respected papa."

"You should thank God that my hands are tied," Dowell replied, "otherwise you would have been sorry. Don't you dare mention my father... bastard!"

"I am very grateful that you are tied up, and for a long time, my dear guest!"

Ravineau turned and left. The lock clicked loudly. Dowell was left alone.

He was not too worried about himself. His friends wouldn't leave him and were bound to get him out of this prison. Still, he realized the danger of his situation. Ravineau had to understand that the outcome of his conflict with Dowell could be detrimental to the fate of his entire enterprise. That was the reason Ravineau halted the conversation abruptly and left. As a good psychologist, he immediately realized who he was dealing with and did not even try applying his inquisition talents. Arthur Dowell could not be defeated through psychology and words, but only through drastic action.

BETWEEN LIFE AND DEATH

Arthur weakened the knots that were restraining him. He managed to do that because when the orderlies were putting the straightjacket on him, he purposely bulged his muscles. He slowly started making his way out of his bindings. However, he was being watched. The moment he attempted getting an arm free, the lock clicked, the door opened, two orderlies entered, and re-wrapped him, adding several leather straps over the straightjacket. The orderlies handled him roughly and threatened to beat him should he renew his attempts to get free. Dowell said nothing. Having finished binding him, the orderlies left.

As there were no windows in the cell and it was lit only by an electric lamp on the ceiling, Dowell did not know whether or not it was already morning. Hours passed slowly. Ravineau did nothing and did not return. Dowell was thirsty. Soon he felt pangs of hunger. But no one entered his cell and brought him food or drink.

"Is he trying to starve me to death?" Dowell thought. Hunger bothered him more and more, but he did not ask for food. If Ravineau was determined to starve him, there was no sense in humiliating himself by asking.

Dowell did not know that Ravineau was testing the strength of his character. Much to Ravineau's displeasure, Dowell had passed this test.

Despite hunger and thirst, Dowell, who hadn't slept in a while, fell asleep. He slept peacefully and deeply, not realizing that he was further annoying Ravineau. Neither the bright light nor Ravineau's musical experiments seemed to have any effect on Dowell. Then Ravineau decided to use stronger methods of influence, which he usually applied to stronger individuals. In the next room, the orderlies started striking iron sheets with wood mallets and spinning special clappers designed to be particularly loud. Even the toughest people woke up at this hellish noise and looked around in terror. But Dowell must have been tougher than tough. He slept like a child. This unusual case impressed even Ravineau.

"Incredible," Ravineau wondered, "this man knows that his life hangs by a thread, but he won't wake up even to the trumpets of archangels."

"Enough!" he shouted to the orderlies, and the hellish music stopped.

Ravineau did not know that the infernal thundering did wake up Dowell. But being a man of strong will, he kept himself in check at the first glimpse of awakening and did not give a single sign that he was no longer asleep.

"Dowell can only be eliminated through physical means," such was Ravineau's conclusion.

When the noise stopped, Dowell fell back asleep and slept till evening. He woke up fresh and rested. Hunger did not feel nearly as strong now. He lay with his eyes open and gazed at the spy-hole in the door with a smile. Someone's round eye was there, watching him carefully.

To tease his enemy a little, Arthur started humming a merry tune. This was too much even for Ravineau. For the first time in his life he felt that he could not control another person's will. A helpless tied up man was making fun of him. There was a hissing sound behind the door. The eye disappeared from the spy-hole.

Dowell continued singing louder, but suddenly choked. Something was irritating his throat. Dowell sniffed and smelled something. His throat and hose itched, and a sharp pain in his eyes followed soon. The smell intensified.

Dowell stopped cold. He realized that this was the end. Ravineau poisoned him with chlorine. Dowell knew that he could not break free of the leather straps and the straightjacket. But at that moment, the instinct of self-preservation was stronger than reason. Dowell started making desperate efforts to free himself. He writhed with his entire body, like a worm, flexed, twisted, rolled from wall to wall. But he did not scream or beg for help, he clenched his teeth and remained silent. His dimmed consciousness no longer controlled his body and defended itself instinctively.

Then the light faded and Dowell felt as if he fell somewhere. He came to from a gust of fresh wind ruffling his hair. With an incredible effort he tried to open his eyes: for a moment he glimpsed Laret's familiar face, but for some reason he was dressed in a police uniform. He heard the noise of a car engine. He had a splitting headache. "I am delusional, but must still be alive," Dowell thought. His eyes closed again, but then flew open.

166

The daylight was painful. Arthur squinted and suddenly heard a woman's voice, "How do you feel?"

Dowell's inflamed eyelids were brushed by a damp piece of cotton. When his vision cleared, Arthur saw Lauran leaning over him. He smiled at her, glanced around and saw that he was in the same room that used to house Briquet.

"I am not dead then?" Dowell asked quietly.

"Fortunately no, although you were but a hair's width from death," Lauran said.

There were quick footsteps in the next room and Arthur saw Laret. His friend was waving his arms and shouting, "I heard voices! He is back to life then. Hello, my friend! How are you doing?"

"Thank you," Dowell replied and felt an ache in his chest. "My head hurts… and my chest…"

"Don't try to talk," Laret warned him, "or you'll hurt yourself. That scoundrel Ravineau nearly poisoned you with gas, like a rat in a ship's hold. But Dowell, we tricked him splendidly!"

And Laret laughed so loudly that Lauran gazed at him reproachfully, concerned that his overly ebullient joy might disturb the patient.

"I know, I know," he said, catching her gaze. "I shall tell you everything as it happened. Having kidnapped Mademoiselle Lauran and waited for you, we realized that you couldn't follow her…"

"Did you… hear my shout?" Arthur asked.

167

"We did. Be quiet! And we hurried to drive away before Ravineau sent out someone to chase us. Struggling with you delayed his posse, and that helped us greatly in getting away unnoticed. We knew very well that you wouldn't be in for a good time there. This was a declaration of war. We, that is Shaub and I, wanted to save you as soon as possible. However, we first had to settle Mademoiselle Lauran and then figure out and plan your rescue. After all, your capture was unforeseen. So, we had to somehow get behind that stone wall and you know how hard that is. Then we decided to do this: Shaub and I managed to get police uniforms, then we drove up and stated that we were there for an inspection. Shaub even managed to produce a mandate with all the proper stamps. Fortunately, the man at the gates was not the usual guard but an orderly, who was apparently unfamiliar with Ravineau's instruction to call him before letting anyone in. We acted with confidence and…"

"Then it wasn't delirium…" Arthur interrupted. "I remember seeing you in police uniform and hearing the car noise."

"Yes, yes, you had a breath of fresh air in the car and came to, but then fainted again. Here is what happened. The orderly opened the gates to us and we entered. The rest was not too difficult, although not as easy as we had hoped. I demanded to be taken to Ravineau's office. But the second orderly we ran into was apparently a more experienced man. He looked us over suspiciously, said he would announce us, and went into the

168

building. In a few minutes some hook-nosed man in horn-rimmed glasses came to see us. He had a white coat on."

"Ravineau's assistant, Doctor Bush."

Laret nodded and continued, "He declared that Doctor Ravineau was busy and that we could discuss our business with him, Bush. I insisted that we had to see Ravineau himself. Bush repeated that it was not possible, as Ravineau was tending to a gravely ill patient. Then Shaub decided we'd waited long enough, grabbed Bush's hand like this," Laret wrapped his right hand around the wrist of his left, "and turned it like this. Bush screamed in pain and we went past him. Damn it, we did not know where Ravineau was and were rather lost. Fortunately, he was walking down the corridor just then. I recognized him because I've seen him before when I dropped off my 'mentally ill friend' – you. 'What do you want?' Ravineau asked. We realized there was no sense in pretending any more, approached Ravineau, pulled out our revolvers, and pointed them at his head. But at that time, that big-nosed Bush – who knew that wimp was so quick! – struck Shaub's hand so strongly and suddenly that he dropped the revolver, and Ravineau grabbed my hand. The fun that followed is hard to describe. Orderlies were running from every direction to help Ravineau and Bush. Fortunately, many of them were taken aback by the uniforms. They knew about heavy penalties for resisting police, especially when said resistance was associated with physical violence against the representatives of the law. No matter how loudly Ravineau yelled that our police uniforms were merely a

169

façade, most orderlies preferred the role of observers, and only a few dared to place their hands upon the sacred and inviolable police jackets.

"Our second trump card was the firearms, which the orderlies did not have. And perhaps our strength, agility and daring helped too. That evened out the odds. One orderly jumped onto Shaub's back as he leaned down to pick up the revolver. Shaub turned out to be a great expert in various forms of combat. He shook off his enemy and, dealing out a few well-placed strikes, kicked away the revolver, just as someone's hand was already reaching for it. I must give him credit, he fought with extreme composure and self-possession. Two more orderlies hung on my shoulders. I don't know what would have happened had it not been for Shaub. He was a hero. He managed to get to his revolver and used it without any delay. Several shots quickly cooled the orderlies' interest. After one of them screamed holding onto his bloodied shoulder, the rest opted to vanish quickly. But Ravineau did not give up. Despite the fact that he had a gun barrel at each temple, he shouted, 'I have weapons too. I shall order my people to shoot, if you don't get out of here immediately!' Then Shaub, without another word, started twisting Ravineau's arm. This trick caused such infernal pain that even the great big burglars and murderers roar like wounded hippos and become sweet and obliging. Ravineau's bones were creaking and there were tears in his eyes, but he still would not give in. 'What are you looking at?' he shouted to the orderlies standing in the distance. 'Go get the

170

guns!' Several of them ran off to his arsenal and the others started approaching us again. I pulled my revolver away from Ravineau's head for a moment and fired a couple of shots. Once again, his servants halted, except for one that fell down groaning…"

Laret drew a breath and continued, "Yes, it was quite a scuffle. Intolerable pain made Ravineau weaker and weaker, and Shaub kept on twisting. Finally Ravineau hissed, 'What do you want?' 'Immediate release of Arthur Dowell,' I said. 'Indeed,' Ravineau replied, gritting his teeth, 'I recognized your face. Let go of my arm, damn it! I shall take you to him…' Shaub let go of the arm, but only just enough to keep him coherent; he was beginning to swoon from pain. Ravineau took us to your cell and pointed at the key. I unlocked the door and entered with Ravineau and Shaub. It was an unhappy sight: you were swaddled like a baby and twisting on the floor like a crushed worm. The cell was filled with suffocating smell of chlorine. Tired of fussing with Ravineau, Shaub dealt him a slight hit in the jaw, which sent the good doctor rolling like a sack. We almost suffocated while dragging you out of the cell, and then we shut the door."

"What about Ravineau? He…"

"If he suffocates, it wouldn't be a great loss, we thought. But he was probably freed and taken care of after we left. We made it out of that hornets' nest fairly easily, except we had to spend our few remaining bullets defending against the dogs. And here you are."

"How long was I unconscious?"

"Ten hours. The doctor has only just left, once your pulse and breathing were back to normal and he felt confident that you were out of danger. Yes, my dear man," Laret said, rubbing his hands, "there are some big trials coming up. Ravineau shall be in court right next to Professor Kern. I won't just let this rest."

"But first we must find my father's head – dead or alive," Arthur said quietly.

WITHOUT A BODY... AGAIN

Professor Kern was so happy about Briquet's unexpected return that he forgot to scold her. Although, she was in plenty of trouble without that. John had to carry Briquet in, with her moaning in pain the entire time.

"Doctor, forgive me," she said to Kern. "I didn't listen to you…"

"And ended up punishing yourself," Kern said, helping John settle the escapee onto the bed.

"My God, I didn't even take off my coat."

"Let me help you with that."

Kern started carefully taking off Briquet's coat, while looking her over with his experienced eye. Her face looked uncommonly young and fresh. There wasn't a trace of wrinkles. "The glands are doing their job," he thought. "Angelica Gaye's young body rejuvenated Briquet's head."

Professor Kern had long since found out whose body he stole from the morgue. He followed the newspapers carefully and chuckled while reading about the search for "vanished" Angelica Gaye.

"Careful… My leg hurts," Briquet winced, when Kern rolled her over on the other side.

"So much for all your jumping around. I have warned you."

The nurse entered. She was an elderly woman with a slightly dimwitted face.

"Undress her," Kern pointed at Briquet.

"Where is Mademoiselle Lauran?" Briquet asked.

"She is not here. She is ill."

Kern turned away, drummed his fingers on the headboard and left the room.

"Have you been working long for Professor Kern?" Briquet asked the new nurse.

The latter hummed and pointed at her mouth.

"She is a mute," Briquet realized. "I won't even have anyone to talk to."

The nurse quietly took away the coat and left. Kern appeared shortly.

"Show me your leg."

"I danced a lot," Briquet began her confession. "And the scratch on the sole opened up again. But I didn't notice…"

"Did you continue dancing?"

"No, it hurt to dance. But then I played tennis. It's such a charming game!"

While Kern listened to Briquet, he carefully examined her leg and became increasingly grim. The leg was swollen up to the knee and turning black. He pressed in several places.

"Ow, it hurts!" Briquet cried out.

"Do you have a fever?"

"Yes, since last night."

"I see…" Kern pulled out a cigar and lit up. "The situation is very grave. This is what happens when you don't listen to me. Who did you play tennis with?"

174

Briquet was embarrassed, "With one... young man."

"Won't you tell me what happened to you since you ran away?"

"I stayed with my friend. She was very surprised to see me alive. I told her that my gunshot wound was not deadly and that I was treated at a hospital."

"Did you say anything about me and... the other heads?"

"Of course not," Briquet replied confidently. "It wouldn't have made any sense. People would have thought I was crazy."

Kern sighed in relief. "It turned out better than I expected," he thought.

"But what is wrong with my leg, Professor?"

"I am afraid I shall have to cut it off."

Briquet's eyes filled with terror.

"Cut off the leg! My leg? You want to make me a cripple?"

Kern himself did not want to disfigure the body obtained and revived with such great difficulties. And the demonstration would not have the same effect if he had to show a cripple. He wished he could avoid the amputation, but it was unlikely.

"Perhaps, you could attach me a new leg?"

"Don't worry, we'll wait until tomorrow. I shall visit you soon," Kern said and left.

The silent nurse came back. She brought a cup of broth and toast. Briquet had no appetite. She was feverish and despite the nurse's persistent gesturing she could eat no more than two spoonfuls.

175

"Take this away, please, I can't."

The nurse left.

"You should have taken her temperature first," Briquet heard Kern's voice from the next room. "Don't you know simple things like that? I told you."

The nurse returned and held out a thermometer to Briquet.

The patient put the thermometer under her arm without any questions. When she pulled it out and checked, it read 102.2 degrees Fahrenheit.

The nurse wrote down the temperature and sat down near the patient.

To avoid seeing the nurse's dumb and unperturbed face, Briquet turned her head to the wall. Even that small movement caused pain in her leg and at the bottom of her stomach. Briquet groaned quietly and closed her eyes. She thought about Laret, "Darling, when shall I see him?"

At nine in the evening the fever increased and Briquet became delirious. Briquet thought she was aboard the yacht. The pitching increased, the yacht was rolling, and a wave of nausea rose in her chest. Laret attacked and tried to strangle her. She screamed and thrashed in bed. Something damp and cold was pressed against her head and chest. The nightmares went away.

Briquet saw herself at the tennis court with Laret. The blue sea rolled beyond the light fence. The sun was mercilessly hot, and she had a headache and felt dizzy. "If only my head didn't hurt.

This sun is terrible! I might miss the ball..." And she carefully watched Laret's movements as he raised his racket for a strike.

"Play!" Laret shouted, his teeth shining in the bright sun, and threw the ball before she had a chance to respond. "Out," Briquet shouted back, happy about Laret's mistake.

"Still playing tennis?" she heard someone's unpleasant voice and opened her eyes. Kern stood over her holding her head and measuring her pulse. He then examined her leg and shook his head in disapproval.

"What time is it?" Briquet asked, barely able to move her tongue.

"It's after one in the morning. Listen, my dear dancer, I must amputate your leg."

"What does that mean?"

"Cut it off."

"When?"

"Now. I cannot delay another hour, otherwise an overall blood poisoning will begin."

Briquet's thoughts were confused. She heard Kern's voice as if in her sleep and barely understood his words.

"How high must you cut it?" she said almost indifferently.

"This high." Kern ran the edge of his hand across her stomach. The gesture chilled Briquet to the bone. Her consciousness cleared.

"No, no, no," she said, terrified. "I won't let you! I don't want to!"

"Do you want to die?" Kern asked calmly.

"No."

"Then make your choice."

"But what about Laret? He loves me," Briquet babbled. "I want to live and be healthy. And you want to take away everything. You are terrible, I am afraid of you! Help! Help me!"

She became delirious once again, started crying and tried to get up. The nurse barely managed to restrain her. Soon, she had to ring for John to help out.

In the meantime, Kern was working quickly in the next room, preparing for surgery.

Exactly at two in the morning Briquet was placed on the operating table. She was lucid and watched Kern silently the way a criminal sentenced to death would watch his executioner.

"Have mercy," she finally whispered. "Save me..."

A mask was pressed to her face. The nurse checked her pulse. John pressed the mask down harder and harder. Briquet fainted.

She came to in bed. She was dizzy and felt nauseous. She remembered the surgery vaguely and, despite terrible weakness, she raised her head to look at her leg and moaned quietly. The leg has been cut off above the knee and tightly bandaged. Kern kept his word: he did everything in his power to disfigure Briquet's body as little as possible. He took a risk and did the surgery in such a way as to make a prosthesis possible.

All day after the surgery Briquet felt satisfactory, although the fever did not go away, which greatly concerned Kern. He visited her every hour to examine her leg.

"What am I going to do now, without a leg?" Briquet asked him.

"Don't worry, I'll make you another leg, better than before," Kern assured her. "You'll dance again." But his face was grim: the leg turned red and swollen above the bandages.

By evening the fever grew worse again. Briquet started thrashing, moaning and became delirious.

At eleven in the evening the temperature rose to 105.1 degrees Fahrenheit.

Kern cursed. It became perfectly clear that the general blood poisoning has begun. Then, no longer thinking about saving Briquet's body, Kern decided to win from death at least some portion of his exhibit. "If I clear her blood vessels first with the antiseptic and then with the physiological solution and run fresh healthy blood through them, the head will live."

He ordered to place Briquet onto the operating table once again.

Briquet was unconscious and did not feel when a sharp scalpel quickly made a cut on her neck, above the red scars from the first surgery. This cut not only separated Briquet's head from her beautiful young body. It separated her from the entire world, all the joys and hopes she lived with.

179

TOMAS DIES FOR THE SECOND TIME

Tomas' head grew more despondent every day. He was unaccustomed to living by brain activity alone. In order to feel good, he needed to work, move, lift heavy things, tire out his strong body, and then eat a lot and sleep well.

He often closed his eyes and imagined straining his back to lift and carry heavy sacks. He thought he could feel every muscle. The sensation was so real that he opened his eyes in hopes to see his body. But there was nothing there but the legs of his stand.

Tomas gritted his teeth and closed his eyes again.

To entertain himself, he thought about his village. But then he would immediately remember his fiancée, who was now lost to him. Many times he asked Kern to give him a new body, but Kern brushed him off, "I haven't found a suitable one yet, be patient."

"At least give me some sickly little body," Tomas asked, so great was his desire to return back to life.

"You won't last for long with a sickly little body. You need a healthy body," Kern replied.

Tomas waited, days followed days, but his head was still stuck on the tall stand.

Particularly difficult were the sleepless nights. He hallucinated. The room spun, fog appeared out of nowhere, and a horse stepped out of it. The sun rose. A dog ran around the yard and the chickens were fussing about. Suddenly, a roaring truck appeared

180

out of nowhere, bearing straight at Tomas. This scene repeated itself endlessly and Tomas died an endless number of times.

To avoid the nightmares, Tomas started whispering songs – he thought he was singing – or counting.

At one point he became amused by one trick. Tomas tried holding the air stream in his mouth. When he opened his mouth, the air burst free with a funny noise.

Tomas liked that and he tried it again. He kept the air until it hissed through his teeth. Tomas tried moving his tongue and found the resulting sounds very funny. For how many seconds could he keep the air in? Tomas started counting. Five, six, seven, eight... "Sh-sh-sh," the air burst free. Again... He wanted to make it to a dozen... One, two, three... six, seven... nine... eleven...twelve...

The compressed air suddenly struck his upper palate with such force that Tomas felt his head rise on its stand.

"Hey, I might fall of my perch," Tomas thought.

He glanced down and saw blood spreading over the glass surface and dripping onto the floor. Apparently, the stream of air, having raised his head had weakened the tubes inserted into the blood vessels of his neck. Tomas head was horrified; was it the end? His consciousness began fading. Tomas felt as if he was running out of air; the blood feeding his head could not longer make it into his brain, providing the life-giving oxygen. He saw his blood flowing away and sensed his slow demise. He didn't want to

181

die! His consciousness clutched at life. To live no matter what! To wait for the new body promised by Kern.

Tomas tried to settle his head back down by contracting his neck muscles, tried rocking back and forth but only made things worse; the glass tips became looser. With one last glint of consciousness, Tomas started screaming, screaming as he never did before in his life.

But it was no longer a scream, but a death rattle.

When John woke up from these strange sounds and ran into the room, Tomas' head barely moved its lips. John settled the head back into place to the best of his ability, inserted the tubes deeper and carefully wiped the blood to make certain that Professor Kern would not find any traces of the night-time incident.

In the morning Briquet's head, separated from her body, was back in its old place, on a metal stand with the glass top, and Kern was slowly waking her up.

Once he "rinsed" the remains of infected blood out of the head and turned on a stream of fresh, healthy blood heated to 98.6 degrees, Briquet's face turned pink. In a few minutes she opened her eyes and, still not understanding, gazed at Kern. She then looked down with an obvious effort and her eyes widened.

"Without a body..." Briquet's head whispered, and here eyes filled with tears. Now she could only hiss: the vocal cords were cut above the old section.

"Excellent," Kern thought, "her system is quickly filling with moisture, unless this is just the residual in her tear ducts. But the precious moisture must not be wasted on tears."

"Don't cry and don't be sad, Mademoiselle Briquet. You have cruelly punished yourself for your own disobedience. But I shall make you a new body, better than before, if only you wait a few days."

Stepping away from Briquet's head, Kern came up to Tomas.

"How is our farmer doing?"

Kern suddenly frowned and looked carefully at Tomas' head. It looked very bad. The skin had darkened and the mouth was half-opened. Kern examined the tubes and turned on John with curses.

"I thought Tomas was asleep," John tried to defend himself.

"You are the one who overslept, idiot!"

Kern started working on the head.

"Ah, how terrible!" Briquet's head hissed. "He is dead. I am so afraid of dead people. I am afraid to die. Why did he die?"

"Close her air valve!" Kern ordered angrily.

Briquet was silenced in mid-word, but continued gazing into the eyes of the nurse with a frightened and pleading expression, helplessly moving her lips.

"If I can't revive the head in twenty minutes, all I can do is throw it away," Kern said.

In fifteen minutes the head showed some signs of life. Its eyelids and lips moved, but its eyes gazed dumbly and

183

senselessly. In another two minutes, the head uttered a few unintelligible words. Kern was ready to celebrate his victory. But the head went quiet again. Not a single muscle moved in its face.

Kern looked at the thermometer, "Corpse temperature. It's over!"

Forgetting Briquet's presence, he irately pulled the head by its thick hair off the stand and tossed it into the large metal basin.

"Take it to the freezer. I shall have to do an autopsy."

The African quickly grabbed the basin and left. Briquet's head watched him with eyes widened in terror.

The phone rang in Kern's study. Kern threw down the cigar he was about to smoke and left, slamming the door behind him.

It was Ravineau. He was calling to tell Kern that he sent him an urgent latter by express mail, which he should receive any moment.

Kern went downstairs and took the letter from the mailbox at the door. While walking up the stairs, Kern nervously tore the envelope open and started reading. Ravineau informed him that Arthur Dowell, having gotten into the clinic disguised as a patient, has kidnapped Mademoiselle Lauran and ran away himself.

Kern missed a step and nearly fell down the stairs.

"Arthur Dowell! Professor's son... He is here? And, of course, he knows everything."

This was a new enemy who would have no mercy on him. Kern burned the letter in the fireplace in his study and paced around the room considering what to do. Should he destroy

Professor Dowell's head? He could do that at any time. But he still needed the head. He had to take measures to make certain that this clue was not seen by any strangers. There could be a search, a visit to his house by his opponents. And so... he had to demonstrate Briquet's head sooner. The victor was always right. No matter what Lauran and Arthur Dowell said, Kern would have an easier time fighting them, after his name was surrounded by the aura of overall admiration and respect.

Kern picked up the phone, called the secretary of a prominent scientific society and asked him to stop by to discuss a presentation at which he, Kern, would demonstrate the results of his most recent research. Then Kern called all the largest newspapers and asked them to send their correspondents.

"We must create as much publicity around Professor Kern's greatest discovery as possible. The demonstration can be conducted in about three days, once Briquet's head has recovered from shock and gotten used to losing the body. And now..."

Kern went into the laboratory, rifled through the various cases, pulled out a syringe, a Bunsen burner, some cotton, and a bottle inscribed "Paraffin" and went to see Professor Dowell's head.

CONSPIRATORS

Laret's house became the headquarters of the conspirators: Arthur Dowell, Laret, Shaub and Lauran. The group decided that it was too risky for Lauran to return to her own apartment. But because Lauran wanted to see her mother as soon as possible, Laret went to get Madam Lauran and brought her to his house.

Seeing her daughter alive and unharmed, the little old woman nearly swooned with joy; Laret had to catch her and sit her down in an armchair.

Mother and daughter were settled in the two third-floor rooms. Madam Lauran's joy was curbed by only one thing – the fact that Arthur Dowell, her daughter's rescuer, was still sick. Fortunately, his body was not under the influence of the poisonous gas for too long. His exceptionally healthy metabolism also helped.

Madam Lauran and her daughter took turns watching the patient. Arthur Dowell grew very fond of the Laurans, and Marie Lauran watched over him with increasing care; unable to help the father, Lauran transferred her attention to the son. Or at least that was what she thought. But there was another reason why she was reluctant to surrender her nursing duties to her mother. Arthur Dowell was the first man to truly impress her. Their meeting took place under romantic circumstances – like a Medieval knight, he rescued her from Ravineau's terrible clinic. The terrible fate of his father lent him an air of tragedy as well. And his personal qualities

– courage, strength and youth—completed the charm, making it difficult to resist.

Arthur Dowell greeted Marie Lauran with an equally tender gaze. He was better equipped to sort out his feelings and did not pretend that his sympathy was merely out of gratitude of a patient toward his attentive nurse.

The exchanges between two young people did not escape the attention of the others. Lauran's mother pretended that she did not notice anything, although she clearly approved of her daughter's choice. Shaub, who was so carried away with sports that he generally ignored women, chuckled mockingly, feeling a little sorry for Arthur. Laret sighed heavily as he watched the dawn of someone else's happiness and remembered Angelica's beautiful body, more often than not imagining it with Briquet's head. He became angry with himself for this "treachery", but justified himself by the law of association: Briquet's head always followed Gaye's body.

Arthur Dowell couldn't wait for the doctor to let him out of bed. But in the meantime, he was only allowed to speak while sitting in bed. All the others were ordered to take care not to task Dowell's lungs.

Willingly or not, he had to assume the role of a chairman, having to listen to other people's opinions and being able only to object or briefly summarize the "debates".

The debates themselves were often tumultuous. Laret and Shaub contributed the greatest share of hot-headedness.

What to do about Ravineau and Kern? For some reason, Shaub chose Ravineau as his favorite victim and kept planning various ways to attack him.

"We didn't have a chance to finish off that hound. And he must be finished off. His every breath makes the world more foul! I won't rest until I strangle him with my own hands. You said," he heatedly addressed Dowell, "that we should leave this business up to a judge and an executioner. But Ravineau himself said that all the government was in his pocket."

"Local government," Dowell said.

"Wait, Dowell," Laret intervened. "You shouldn't talk. And you, Shaub, are becoming a distracter. We will always have time to do away with Ravineau. Our primary goal must be uncovering Kern's crimes and locating Professor Dowell's head. We must find a way to get into Kern's house."

"But how are you going to do that?" Arthur asked.

"How? The way burglars do."

"But you are not a burglar. That too is an art, and a serious one at that."

Laret thought about it, then clapped himself on the forehead. "We can invite Jean. Briquet told me, as a friend, the secret of his profession. He shall be flattered! For the first time in his life he shall break into someone's house for a noble cause."

"What if he is not all that noble?"

"We shall pay him. He can let us in and vanish from the scene before we call the police, which we will have to do."

His ardor was cooled by Arthur Dowell. Quietly and slowly he started talking, "I think that all this romantic stuff is unnecessary in this case. Kern probably already knows from Ravineau about my arrival to Paris and my participation in Mademoiselle Lauran's kidnapping. Besides, I am the son of… the late Professor Dowell and have a legal right, as a lawyer would say, to open a case and demand a criminal investigation and a search."

"You are speaking legalese again," Laret flapped his hand hopelessly. "These legal people will only confuse you and Kern will get away."

Arthur coughed and winced at the pain in his chest.

"You talk too much," Madam Lauran, who sat next to Arthur, said anxiously.

"It's nothing," he said, rubbing his chest. "It will go away soon…"

At that moment Marie Lauran entered the room, clearly agitated by something.

"Here, read this," she said, holding out a newspaper to Dowell.

A bold title on the first page announced, "PROFESSOR KERN'S SENSATIONAL DISCOVERY."

The smaller sub-title said, "Demonstration of a revived human head."

The following article said that the following evening Professor Kern would give a lecture to the scientific community. The lecture would be followed by the demonstration of a living human head.

The announcement was followed by the history of Kern's research, a listing of his scientific publications and his most famous surgeries.

Under the first article was a larger one, signed by Kern himself. In it, he outlined the history with reviving the heads, starting with dogs and then moving on to people.

Lauran alternated between watching the expression of Arthur Dowell's face and the movement of his eyes as they went from one line to the next. Dowell kept outwardly calm. Only when he finished reading, a sad smile flickered across his face.

"Is this not outrageous?" Marie Lauran exclaimed, when Arthur silently returned the newspaper to her. This scoundrel doesn't say a single word about your father's role in this entire 'sensational discovery'. No, I cannot just leave it like this!" Lauran's cheeks were flushed. "Kern must be punished for everything he did to me, to your father, to you, to those unfortunate heads he resurrected for the hell of a bodiless existence. He must be held accountable not only to the law, but also to the society. It would be the greatest injustice to allow him to triumph even for an hour."

"What do you want?" Dowell asked quietly.

"To ruin his triumph!" Lauran replied passionately. "To show up at the meeting and publicly accuse Kern of being a murderer and a thief."

Madam Lauran was seriously concerned. Only now did she realize how greatly her daughter's nerves had been compromised. This was the first time she saw her gentle, self-possessed

190

daughter in such agitated state. Madam Lauran tried calming her down, but the girl seemed not to notice anything around her. She was burning with indignation and desire of revenge. Laret and Shaub watched her with surprise. Her impatience and indomitable anger surpassed their own. Lauran's mother glanced pleadingly at Arthur Dowell. He caught her gaze and said, "Your actions, Mademoiselle Lauran, driven as it is by noble intentions, is irra..."

But Lauran interrupted him, "There are forms of irrationality that are worthier than wisdom. Don't think that I want to play the role of a heroic accuser. But I cannot act any other way. My own moral code requires it."

"But what will you achieve? You can't tell all this to a police detective?"

"No, I want Kern to be publicly disgraced! He is building his fame on the other's misfortunes, on a foundation of crime and murder! Tomorrow he wants to reap his laurels. I only want him to reap what he deserves."

"I oppose this, Mademoiselle Lauran," Arthur Dowell said, afraid that Lauran's performance might have too serious an impact on her nerves.

"It is a pity," she replied. "But I would not abandon this plan, even if the entire world was against me. You don't know me!"

Arthur Dowell smiled. He liked this youthful zeal, and he liked Marie herself with her flashing eyes and glowing cheeks even better.

"This would be a very ill-advised step," he reasoned again. "You are subjecting yourself to a great risk…"

"We shall protect her!" Laret exclaimed, raising his arm as if he was holding a rapier and prepared to strike.

"Yes, we shall protect you," Shaub loudly supported his friend shaking his fist.

Marie Lauran, encouraged by this support, looked at Arthur reproachfully.

"In that case, I too shall accompany you," he said.

Joy flickered through Lauran's eyes, followed by a frown.

"You can't… You are still unwell."

"I shall go anyway."

"But…"

"And I would not abandon this plan, even if the entire world was against me. You don't know me," he repeated her own words with a smile.

A RUINED TRIUMPH

On the day of his presentation, Kern examined Briquet head with particular care.

"Listen," he said, having finished the examination. "Tonight at eight you shall be taken to a large gathering. You will have to talk. Answer the questions briefly. Don't say anything extra. Do you understand?"

Kern opened the air valve, and Briquet whispered, "I do, but I would like to... please..."

Kern left without listening to her.

His anxiety grew. He had a difficult task ahead – to deliver the head to the scientific assembly building. The smallest push could be fateful to the head's life.

A specially equipped car was prepared. The head's stand with all the equipment was placed on a special cart with wheels for rolling across the floor and handles for carrying up the stairs. Finally, everything was ready. They were underway at seven in the evening.

The enormous white hall was flooded with bright light. The parterre was filled with gray and shiny bald heads of the old scientists dressed in black tuxedoes and suits. Light glinted off their gold glasses and monocles. The boxes and amphitheater were filled with an assorted audience of individuals who had some connection with the scientific world.

The gorgeous gowns and glittering diamonds of the ladies brought to mind a concert hall during performances by world-known celebrities.

The subdued hum filled the hall as the spectators waited for the presentation to begin.

The newspaper correspondents fussed at their small tables near the stage, like a bunch of busy ants, sharpening their pencils and setting out their notepads for stenographic recording.

Off to the right was a series of movie cameras to capture on film every aspect of Kern's performance, especially the revived head. On stage there was a large table where the most prominent representatives of science were seated. A lectern stood in the middle of the stage. The microphone was wired to broadcast the lecture to radio stations around the world. The second microphone stood in front of Briquet's head. She was placed stage left. A skillfully applied subdued makeup made Briquet's head look fresh and attractive, smoothing the difficult impression she would make on unprepared spectators. The nurse and John stood near her table.

Marie Lauran, Arthur Dowell, Laret and Shaub sat in the front row, two paces away from the stage. Shaub was the only one who did not need to change his appearance. Lauran wore an evening gown and veiled hat. She kept her head low to make certain that Kern could not recognize her. Arthur Dowell and Laret showed up in makeup with skillfully applied beards and mustache. For greater secrecy they decided to pretend that they did not know each other. They sat silently, casting an occasional indifferent glance at their neighbors. Laret was profoundly depressed – he almost collapsed at the sight of Briquet's head.

Exactly at eight, Professor Kern stepped up to the lectern. He looked paler than usual but very dignified.

The audience greeted him with a long round of applause.

The movie cameras hummed. The newspaper anthill went silent. Professor Kern began his lecture about his non-existent discoveries.

The speech was brilliantly composed and perfectly structured. Kern remembered to mention the preliminary, very valuable works of the prematurely dead Professor Dowell. But even as he gave credit to the works of the late professor, he did not forget his own "modest contribution". The audience could have no doubt that the entire honor of the discovery belonged to him, Professor Kern.

His speech was interrupted by applause several times. Hundreds of ladies peered at him through binoculars and lorgnettes, while the men leveled their binoculars and monocles at Briquet's head who was smiling tensely.

At Professor Kern's sign, the nurse opened the valve for the air flow and Briquet's head received the ability to speak.

"How do you feel?" a little old scientist asked her.

"Very well, thank you,"

Briquet's voice was dull and hoarse, the strong air stream whistled, and the sound was almost devoid of modulations, but the head's performance made an incredible impression. Even the

195

world's best performers rarely heard such thunderous applause. But Briquet, who once enjoyed the success of her performances at small bars, only lowered her eyelids.

Lauran's anxiety increased. She started shaking and had to clench her teeth to keep them from chattering. "Now," she told herself several times, but every time she lost her nerve. The environment was oppressive to her. After every missed opportunity she tried to calm herself by the thought that the higher Professor Kern was elevated, the lower his downfall shall be.

Speeches followed.

The little old man who spoke to Briquet and was one of the greatest scientists in the world approached the podium.

In a weak, crackling voice he spoke about Professor Kern's brilliant discovery, about the omnipotence of science, about defeating death, and about the happiness of interacting with the minds that gave the world some of the greatest scientific achievements.

At that moment, when Lauran expected it the least, a whirlwind of long-restrained rage and hatred swept her up. She could not control herself.

She dashed to the podium, nearly knocking the astonished old man off his feet, took his place and, with a deathly pale face and the feverishly flashing eyes of a fury pursuing a murderer, began her passionate if disjointed speech.

The entire audience seemed to wake up at the sight of her.

At the first moment, Professor Kern was taken aback and made a motion toward Lauran, as if wanting to hold her back. He then turned to John and quickly whispered a few words to him. John slipped out through the side door.

No one noticed this in the midst of the overall confusion.

"Do not believe him!" Lauran shouted, pointing at Kern. "He is a thief and a murderer! He stole Professor Dowell's work! He killed Professor Dowell! He still works with the professor's head. He forces it to continue scientific experiments by torture, and then pretends that these are his discoveries. Dowell himself told me that Kern poisoned him."

The confusion in the audience grew into panic. Many people jumped up from their seats. Several reporters dropped their pencils and were frozen in odd poses. Only the cameraman kept running the camera, happy to have this unexpected publicity stunt that would ensure sensational success of his documentary.

Professor Kern was fully in control of himself. He stood calmly, with a smile of pity on his face. When Lauran choked due to a nervous spasm, he took advantage of the pause, turned to the ushers and said to them, "Take her away! Don't you see she is mad?'

The ushers ran to Lauran. But before they managed to get to her through the crowd, Laret, Shaub, and Dowell ran up to her and took her out into the hallway. Kern followed the group with a suspicious gaze.

In the hallway, police tried to detain Lauran but her escorts managed to get her out of the building and get her into the car. They left.

When the hubbub receded, Professor Kern came back to the podium and apologized to the audience for the "unfortunate incident".

"Mademoiselle Lauran is a nervous girl who is prone to hysteria. She could not stand the shock she experienced every day, spending time in the company of Briquet's head I revived. Lauran's psyche cracked. She went mad."

This speech was met by the audience's stunned silence.

Someone tried to clap, but was hissed at. It was as if a wind of death flew over the hall. Hundreds of eyes now looked at Briquet's head with terror and pity, as if she was a ghost. The mood of the audience was hopelessly ruined. Many left without waiting for the conclusion. The speeches prepared in advance were read out quickly, as were the congratulatory telegrams and orders about electing Professor Kern a member and an honorary professor of various universities and academies. Then the meeting ended.

The African appeared behind Professor Kern and, having nodded to him, started preparing Briquet's head for the return trip. The head looked faded, tired and frightened.

Alone in his car, Professor Kern gave way to his anger. He clenched his fist, gritted his teeth and cursed so loudly that the driver had to slow down the car and ask through the communication window, "Hello, everything alright?"

THE LAST MEETING

In the morning following Kern's ill-fated performance, Arthur Dowell came to the chief of police, identified himself and requested a search of Kern's home.

"Professor Kern's home has already been searched last night," the chief replied dryly. "The search yielded no results. Mademoiselle Lauran's statement, as one might have expected, turned out to be nothing but a product of her disturbed imagination. Have you not read about it in the morning papers?"

"Why were you so quick to assume that Mademoiselle Lauran's statement was due to her imagination?"

"Because, as you ought to see for yourself," the chief of police replied, "this sort of thing is completely impossible, and besides, the search has proven..."

"Did you ask the head of Mademoiselle Briquet for her testimony?"

"No, we did not question any heads," the chief of police replied.

"Pity! She could have confirmed having seen the head of my father. She told me about it personally. I insist on another search."

"I have no reasons to do so," the chief of police said harshly.

"Has he been bribed by Kern?" Arthur thought.

"Besides," the chief of police continued, "another search could only cause a public outcry. The public is already sufficiently outraged by the statement of this insane Lauran. Professor Kern is all anyone speaks about. He received hundreds of letters and telegrams with expressions of support for him and indignation about Lauran's actions."

"Nevertheless, I insist that Kern committed several crimes."

"You cannot make such accusations without proof," the chief of police said didactically.

"Then give me an opportunity to obtain proof," Dowell objected.

"You have already had this opportunity. We have conducted a search."

"If you absolutely refuse, I shall be forced to appeal to the county prosecutor," Arthur said blankly and rose.

"There is nothing I can do for you," the chief of police replied and also rose.

The mention of the prosecutor, however, had its effect. After a brief pause, he said, "I could give an order for another search, but unofficially, so to speak. If the search yields new results, I shall report the case to the prosecutor."

"The search must be conducted in the presence of Mademoiselle Lauran and my friend Armand Laret."

"Aren't you asking a bit much?"

"No, these people can be of significant help."

The chief of police spread his hands, sighed and said, "Fine! I shall give several police officers to assist you. I shall also invite an investigator."

At eleven in the morning Arthur was already ringing the bell at Kern's door.

John slightly opened the heavy oak door but did not take off the chain.

"Professor Kern is not seeing anyone."

A police officer stepped forward and ordered John to let the unexpected guests into the house.

Professor Kern met them at his study with the air of insulted virtue.

"Please, come in," he said icily, opening the doors of the laboratory and casting a withering glance at Lauran.

The investigator, Lauran, Arthur Dowell, Kern, Laret, and two policemen entered.

Lauran felt agitated by the environment associated with so many difficult experiences. Her heart beat faster.

Briquet's head was the only one in the lab. Her cheeks without rouge had the dark-yellow color of a mummy. Seeing Lauran and Laret, she smiled and blinked. Laret turned away with a shudder of horror.

They entered the room adjacent to the laboratory.

It contained a shaved head of a middle-aged man with an enormous fleshy nose. The head's eyes were completely concealed by dark glasses. Its lips twitched slightly.

"His eyes are bothering him..." Kern explained. "This is all I can offer you," he added with an ironic smile.

Indeed, the subsequent search of the house, from basement to attic, revealed no other heads.

On the way back, they once again had to go through the room with the big-nosed head. The disappointed Dowell was just about to walk through the next door, followed by the investigator and Kern.

"Wait," Lauran stopped them.

She came up to the head with the big nose, opened the air valve and asked, "Who are you?"

The head moved its lips, but there was no sound. Lauran turned up the air flow.

There was a hissing noise, "Who is that? Is that you, Kern? Unplug my ears! I can't hear you..."

Lauran checked the head's ears and pulled out thick balls of cotton.

"Who are you?" she repeated the question.

"I was Professor Dowell."

"But your face?" Lauran gasped.

"Face?" the head was speaking with difficulty. "Yes, I was deprived of everything, even my face. A little surgery... some paraffin injected under the skin of my nose. Alas, the only thing that is mine is my brain in this disfigured box. But even it refuses to serve me. I am dying... and our experiments are still incomplete... although my head had lived longer than I calculated theoretically."

"What are the glasses for?" the investigator asked, coming closer.

"My colleague doesn't trust me lately," and the head attempted to smile. "He limits my ability to see and hear... The glasses are opaque... to make certain that I don't betray myself before the undesirable visitors. Please remove them."

Lauran took off the glasses with shaking hands.

"Mademoiselle Lauran, is it you? Hello, my dear friend! Kern told me that you left. I feel poorly, I can't work anymore. Kern had informed me of my amnesty only yesterday. If I don't die on my own today, he promised to set me free tomorrow."

Suddenly the head noticed Arthur who was standing off to the side, frozen on the spot without a hint of color in his face, and said happily, "Arthur! Son!"

For a moment, the dull eyes became clear.

"Father, my dear!" Arthur stepped toward the head. "What has he done to you?"

He staggered. Laret supported him.

"It's... good... We got to see each other one more time... after my death..." Professor Dowell's head wheezed.

His vocal cords almost weren't working and his tongue moved poorly. During the frequent pauses, air whistled noisily through his throat.

"Arthur, please kiss me on the forehead, only if it is not... unpleasant... to you."

Arthur leaned forward and kissed the head.

"Right… all is well now…"

"Professor Dowell," the investigator said, can you tell us about the circumstances of your death?"

The head's fading gaze shifted to the investigator, as if not quite understanding the question. Then it pointed at Lauran with its eyes and whispered, "I told her… She knows everything."

The head's lips stopped moving and its eyes became dull.

"Well," the investigator interrupted the heavy silence and said, turning to Kern, "Please follow me to the study! I must obtain your testimony."

When the door closed, Arthur dropped onto a chair next to his father's head and covered his face, "My poor, poor father!"

Lauran gently put her hand on his shoulder. Arthur rose and squeezed her hand firmly.

A gunshot sounded from Kern's study.

ABOUT THE AUTHOR

Alexander Romanovich Belyaev was born in 1884 in Smolensk, in the family of a Russian Orthodox minister. His sister Nina and brother Vasily both died young and tragically.

Following the wishes of his father, Alexander graduated the local seminary but decided not to become a minister. On the contrary, he graduated a passionate atheist. After the seminary he entered a law school in Yaroslavl. When his father died unexpectedly, Alexander had to find ways to make ends meet including tutoring, creating theater sets and playing violin in a circus orchestra.

Fortunately, his law studies did not go to waste. As soon as Belyaev graduated the law school, he established a private practice in his home town of Smolensk and soon acquired a reputation of a talented and shrewd attorney. He took advantage of the better income to travel, acquire a very respectable art collection and create a large library. Belyaev felt so secure, financially, that he got married and left his law practice to write full-time.

At the age of thirty-five Belyaev was faced with the most serious trial of his life. He became ill with Plevritis which, after an unsuccessful treatment attempt, developed into spinal tuberculosis and leg paralysis. His wife left him, unwilling to be tied to a sick man. Belyaev spent six years in bed, three of which – in a full-torso cast. Fortunately, the other two women in his life –

his mother and his old nanny – refused to give up on him. They helped seek out specialists who could help him and took him away from the dismal climate of central Russia to Yalta – a famous Black Sea resort.

While at the hospital in Yalta, Belyaev started writing poetry. He also determined that, while he could not do much with his body, he had to do something with his mind. He read all he could find by Jules Verne, H.G. Wells and by the famous Russian scientist Tsiolkovsky. He studied languages, medicine, biology, history, and technical sciences.

No one had a clear idea how, but in 1922 Belyaev finally overcame his illness and returned to normal life and work. To cut the cost of living, Belyaev moved his family from the expensive Yalta to Moscow and took up law once again. At the same time, he put all the things he learned during the long years of his illness to use, by weaving them into fascinating adventure and science fiction plots. His works appeared more and more frequently in scientific magazines, quickly earning him the title of "Soviet Jules Verne".

After successfully publishing several full-length novels, he moved his family to St. Petersburg (then Leningrad) and once again became a full-time writer. Sadly, the cold damp climate had caused a relapse in Belyaev's health. Unwilling to jeopardize his family's finances by moving to yet another resort town, he compromised by moving them somewhat further south, where the cost of living was still reasonable – to Kiev.

The family didn't get to enjoy the better climes for long. In 1930 the writer's six-year old daughter died of meningitis, his second daughter contracted rickets, and his own illness once again grew worse.

The following years were full of ups and downs. There was the meeting with one of Belyaev's heroes – H.G. Wells n 1934. There was the parting of ways with the magazine *Around the World* after eleven years of collaboration. There was the controversial article *Cinderella* about the dismal state of science fiction at the time.

Shortly before the Great Patriotic War (June 22, 1941 – May 9, 1945), Alexander Romanovich went through yet another surgery and could not evacuate when the war began. The town of Pushkin, a St. Petersburg suburb, where Belyaev and his family lived, became occupied by the German troops. Belyaev died of hunger in January, 1942. A German general and four soldiers took his body away and buried it somewhere. It was highly irregular for the members of the German military to bury a dead Soviet citizen. When asked about it the general explained that he used to enjoy Belyaev's books as a boy, and considered it his duty to bury him properly.

The exact place of Belyaev's burial is unknown to this day. After the war, the Kazan cemetery of the town of Pushkin received a commemorative stele as the sign of remembrance and respect for the great author.

ABOUT THE TRANSLATOR

Maria K. is the pen name of Maria Igorevna Kuroshchepova – a writer, translator, and blogger of Russian-Ukrainian decent. Maria came to the United States in 1994 as an impressionable 19-year old exchange student. She received her Bachelors and Masters degrees in engineering from Rochester Institute of Technology (Rochester, NY).

Maria covers a wide range of topics from travel and fashion to politics and social issues. Her science fiction and fantasy works include Limited Time for Tomato Soup, The SHIELD, The Elemental Tales and others.

A non-fiction and science fiction writer in her own right, Maria is also a prolific translator of less-known works of Russian and Soviet literature into English. Her most prominent translations include her grandfather Vasily Kuznetsov's Siege of Leningrad journals titled The Ring of Nine, and Thais of Athens – a historic novel by Ivan Yefremov. Both works quickly made their way into the top 100 Kindle publications in their respective categories and continue attracting consistent interest and acclaim from readers.